# Gifts

## Bittersweet Christmas Stories

Hadley Colt • David Hogan •
Sam Hawken • Richard
Kalich • Jackie Mallon •
Donald Finnaeus Mayo •
Craig McDonald • Colin
O'Sullivan • Kevin Stevens

Edited by
Svetlana Pironko

BETIMES BOOKS

First published in the English language worldwide in 2014 by
Betimes Books
www.betimesbooks.com

"Slay Belles" © 2014 by Hadley Colt
"Feliz Navidad" © 2014 by Sam Hawken
"Cherry Pink and Apple Blossom White" © 2014 by David Hogan
"The Party" © 2005 by Richard Kalich
"Blue and Unassuming under a Christmas Star" © 2014 by
Jackie Mallon
"No Truce for Christmas" © 2014 by Donald Finnaeus Mayo
"Echoes" © 2010 by Craig McDonald
"Be Good for Goodness Sake" © 2014 by Colin O'Sullivan
"The Return of Eddie Sloan" © 2014 by Kevin Stevens
The collection © Betimes Books
Cover art © Gérard Ramon

Cover design by JT Lindroos

ISBN: 978-0-9929674-4-4

# TABLE OF CONTENTS

# SLAY BELLES

## Hadley Colt

### Author's note

My new novel, *Permanent Fatal Error*, revolves around a presumed-dead author famous for avoiding the limelight, evoking comparisons to J.D. Salinger or Thomas Pynchon. When a noted biographer is hired to pen the late-Everett Hyde's estate-authorized biography, terrible events begin to unfold.

There is also a rather darkly humorous eye cast on the state of publishing, the perils of the writing life, and some of the more extreme personalities who inform the New York City literary scene.

Two of those rather unusual people return in the following story: the fearsome Selma Lindscott, a feral literary agent nicknamed "The Hyena", and her client, retired Navy Seal Robert "Ace" Sterling.

Set a few months after the events of *Permanent Fatal Error*, the uneasy duo return a final time for this very special Yuletide short.

—Hadley Colt

---

Robert "Ace" Sterling, six-five, broad-shouldered and deep-chested, stared at himself in the costume shop mirror, loathing what looked back. He said, "Don't you have, ya know, some kind of Athletic Fit version of this get-up?" Ace's gaze drifted hopefully toward a muscle-bound Batman suit in the corner.

The shop's owner, sixty-something, short and, to Ace's eye, clearly light in the loafers, curled his lip. "Sir, *Kris Kringle*, that is to say *Santa Claus*, is by tradition a short and rotund elf. Candidly, you're already testing credulity on the part of the kiddies as you're essentially going to be playing Santa as, *you know*, an NBA player or some freak with a hyperactive pituitary gland."

The fussy little man took several steps back and eyed the giant in the Santa suit. He clucked his tongue. "I've really done all that I can possibly do with you."

For his part, the giant checked himself again in the tri-panel mirror and sighed.

The costume shop owner—had he said his name was Justin?—sighed too. He said a last time, "That's truly all I can do, sir. Let's just be thankful we somehow had a Santa suit in extra-tall."

Scowling, Ace gave himself a final check in the mirror. The retired Navy Seal, now men's adventure author, worked *so* hard to maintain his body, even keeping chemical fortification to the barest minimum in favor of pumping real iron for *earned* muscle mass.

But now, in this silly plush suit, he looked like some kind of scarlet Bigfoot with a beer gut. The white wig made his shaven head itch and the white beard tickled his real goatee that Ace weekly and painstakingly dyed with Just for Men's shade of "natural black" to prevent exactly this shade of ashen beard from ever sprouting on his true face.

*Jesus Christ,* he thought, *the sorry-ass things I do for that haughty, paranoid bitch.*

That *haughty paranoid bitch* was Ace Sterling's present literary agent, one Selma Lindscott, an ivory-skinned, rail-thin witch on *do-me* heels who other agents and throngs of terrorized authors had dubbed "The Hyena" in New York City literary circles. Selma had picked up Ace and his macho backlist in a fire-sale when his former agent, the man who'd launched Ace's "Iron Seal" series of thrillers, had unexpectedly dropped dead during the long walk from one end to the other of Book Expo ought-seven.

That lethal stroll had been a nasty turn for agent, Bob Gallagher, of course, but it was arguably a worse one for client, Ace, who was still living with the consequences. Representing his literary holdings didn't seem to be enough for Selma. The Hyena also regarded Ace as her personal bodyguard and too-frequently-called-upon mercenary. Take this sorry gig tonight, as evidence.

The big novelist settled up for his costume rental, then realized the damn Santa suit didn't even have simple pockets for his wallet or car keys.

Cursing and still in full Santa mode, Ace stepped out into the fierce winter wind. His free hand immediately went to his head to keep his red velvet hat and long white wig in place. Children pointed and squealed, but kept a wary distance. It was clear to Ace that the kids, and even their fetching MILFs, had never seen old Kris Kringle look so *imposing*, let alone so pissed off.

Once he was safely out of the wind and back inside his gun-metal Hummer, Ace doffed the hat and wig. He slung that itchy white beard into the backseat. He again surveyed the Santa costume, ruing its lack of pockets or means of easy reach under its red coat.

Given his very reason for needing the disguise, and his attendant obligation to escort Selma to her misbegotten agency Christmas party, Ace desperately needed to find some way to pack a piece for swift and easy access. Looking down, he settled on his right, fur-topped Santa boot. Yes, an ankle holster would work well enough. Then he looked at his big red mittens and tore them off. That part of his costume he'd simply have to forego: a man couldn't pull a trigger wearing big crimson elf mittens; there was simply no damned way to do that.

Grinding his teeth, Ace waited out another passing throng of kids and parents, the tykes all red cheeks, runny noses and giggles. Once they were clear, he edged his big SUV into traffic.

Christmas: *Fa-la-la-la-la*, goddamit. This particular holiday was never much of an event for a committed bachelor like Ace.

Most December twenty-fifths found him haunting a Gotham Chinese restaurant – most often he'd land in Wo Hop. There, he'd try (and sometimes even succeed) in picking up some comely, dark-haired, dark-eyed young woman of *that persuasion*: a pretty thing trying to wait out the Christian holiday until the city reopened and dining options once more widened.

It wasn't the worst way to spend a Christmas day and night, and the resulting dubious hook-ups rarely lingered much past New Year's Eve.

A fresh blast of horns made Ace set aside his holiday carnal reveries and focus on the traffic. Rockefeller Plaza was the usual tangle of tourists; all the would-be ice skaters falling on their asses and spraining wrists.

Ace checked his console's clock: he was already fifteen minutes late.

Selma would be all over him for that, of course. She'd been increasingly curt to him. She was also slower these months to return emails and often dodged his calls.

His agent had portentously warned him for some time now that his niche of the book market was narrowing. He sensed her agency focus was shifting even more toward women's books, to more celebrity tell-alls and True Crime stuff.

If she didn't need him for strong-arm stuff like this, and that crazy thing last year with the hot young female writer, Ashley McKnight, Ace sensed Selma might already have cut him loose.

Characteristically, Selma skipped using her seatbelt because she didn't want to *wreck* her *ensemble*. She instead kept one hand pressed to the dash while clutching a Solo cup in the other. It was filled to the brim with a sweet-smelling mix of scant ice, copious white wine and a drizzle of Perrier. ("I will not," she vowed, "suffer even my own agency's Christmas party stone cold sober. Always best to arrive lit, no pun intended.")

Dodging brown-skinned cabbies and their darting yellow sleds, Ace freshly cursed and flipped some Muslim cab driver the bird. He said, "You've been getting threatening letters from that "EH" character for months, now. You ignore those, and life goes on just dandy. What makes *this* threat so different? Why take *this* one seriously?"

"Because I just learned two of my so-called peers, Liddy Dodds and Felicia Cooper, both died last week, and I mean vi-*o*-*lent*-ly," Selma said. "Liddy was stabbed to death with a Hugo Award gifted her by a client. Killed in front of her own staff by a *husky*, masked *man* posing as a delivery man.

Felicia was killed by a *husky woman*, some said maybe a man dressed as a big-boned woman, at a client's book signing. The killer drove a fountain pen into her jugular, then fled before he could be captured. Felicia bled out, right there, in Barnes & Noble, of all sorry places. That is to further say, she died in the fucking *Bronx*." Selma shivered. "I'm told through channels they were both left a threatening phone message just before they died, a message just like the one I received yesterday."

*That message*: Selma had recorded a copy onto her iPhone and emailed it to Ace.

A male voice, low and threatening, warned, "I'm tired of the so-called publishing *business*. I'm sick of the name game and all of the *it's who you know or are* and *not what you write* bullshit. I'm finished with not having my talent or novels recognized for what they are. You and those like you have unfairly killed my prospects with your lack of taste, so I'm going to *kill you*, then shove one of your own form rejection letters down your well-traveled throat, you monstrous old slut. You wouldn't know good writing if it fell on you."

Selma had conceded to Ace yesterday, after she'd announced the threat to him, that form rejection letters *were* probably a mistake, of sorts. "It's maybe off the present point," she'd said, "but from now on, I'm going to have my girl at least insert *something* about the manuscript title and the author's name into my standard rejection slips. If nothing else, it could help the police or some detective later if, well, *you know…*"

Now Ace tugged at the furry white Santa collar freshly tickling his throat and said, "And have you actually called the cops, like I told you to?"

"Yes, but they aren't useful at all, not a lick," Selma said. "They agreed to drive by my place a few extra times a day, and to place calls—*welfare checks*, they actually called them, to me three times a day to make sure I'm not murdered or kidnapped or something. But what good really is any of *that*? Besides, I have enough trouble keeping my cell phone charged, ringing off the hook as it always seems to be. And anyway, I have *The Iron Seal* as my client, and aren't we both lucky for that? So, lover, you just play Santa, but keep an eye peeled. This is killing several birds with one stone, so to speak."

"What do you mean by that?"

Selma patted his thigh. "I get my Santa for my party, you get to enjoy a little holiday cheer with all the kids, and, if something happens, you're there to set it all right. It's win-win, all around, yes?"

"Sure, baby," Ace said, voice going to gravel. "Sure, Selma. It's all that good stuff, for certain."

Selma sat down her nearly drained wine spritzer long enough to help Ace adjust his hat and beard. Waving a bony finger in his face, she lectured, "Stop looking surly. Santa is supposed to be, oh, I don't know, *fun* somehow. Be nice. You'd *better* be fucking jolly, because I won't have all my employees' kids disappointed and my workers bitching all year about what a downer Christmas party I threw. Remember to smile, and I mean, *smile broad-ly.*" Her strident voice echoed in the dimly lit parking garage.

*Smile broadly. Jesus, but you're one to talk*, he thought. Selma had obviously sprung for another Botox treatment, as her typically expressionless face looked more immobile than ever. Ace thought at this moment he couldn't have put a smile on her alabaster mug, not even with the aid of a hydraulic jack.

Selma drained her cup and flung it to the pavement. She looked around and said softly, "You *do* have a gun, don't you?"

"Rod's in my right boot," he said matter-of-factly. "Got throwing knives up either sleeve and a dandy machete down my back." Saying that made Ace feel more himself. He smiled, and *broadly*. "So we're *good*."

She took his arm and said, "Then c'mon, Kris, let's get this holiday hot mess over with." She suddenly stopped walking. "Oh, and after, do you have any screwing partners in queue for this evening? If not, I'm thinking this could be one of our occasional agent-client-with-benefits kinds of nights. What say you to *that*?"

He shrugged, his heart, and the rest of him, not really into it. But covering his options, Ace said softly, "Suppose naughty might be nice."

The agency's offices had been festooned with twinkling lights and a hastily decorated artificial tree occupied the center of the conference room. A bar had been set up near Selma's personal office, and desks had been pushed together to serve as a banquet table.

Throngs of employees, publicists and lit bloggers mingled over free drinks and canapés. One of the bloggers, a bespectacled, bird-like young woman with hipster frames said, "Golly, I wish he *had* jumped off the damned bridge. I think we all wish that."

About a dozen kids were off in a corner, playing X-Box and occasionally stealing wary glances at the towering, strapping Santa making the rounds of fetching young women, a Seven-and-Seven in his left hand. The back of the giant Santa's hand was matted with black hair. It was a jarring sight held up against that snowy white beard, already just a tad stained with whiskey and cola.

As he tried to find some better candidate to pass the later evening with, Santa-Ace also kept a close eye on Selma, presently chatting up a pair of old geezers from two of the surviving Big Five Publishers. The decrepit literary lions looked too frail to pose a threat to anybody. Indeed, on closer inspection, it struck Santa-Ace that something as simple as a Dyson Airblade might constitute a lethal risk to either of the rickety codgers.

More overheard literary back-chatter further set the disguised author's teeth on edge.

A svelte young Latina, some publicist or editor from St. Martin's said, "I told her, 'For God's sake, *don't... you... do... it!* There are already too many photos out there, and a simple Google image search will put the lie to this 'It's all just healthier living' bullshit. 'You don't want,' I told her, 'to end up like poor Olivia Goldsmith, *do you?*'"

Two skinny young men, both wearing studiously knotted and dangling scarves, commiserated about some packaging and design issue. The one said, "But I explicitly stipulated deckle-edge!"

Ace spied no loners, saw no mad-eyed hangers-on.

*No real threat in sight*, Ace decided. He checked his watch: just thirty minutes to go until he was supposed to plant his ass in some chair and let those grubby little kids sit on his knee. Then he was to pass out presents to them. Only after, he was permitted to briefly duck out to become himself.

It was going to be longest hour of his life, he feared.

When the promised threat to Selma was at last delivered upon, it came in a rush.

A husky young bald dude sidled into the party, trying not to draw attention. But he caught Ace's eye immediately. The strapping Santa gently slid a kid off his leg and deftly reached for his four-inch barreled Python.

Simultaneously, Selma waved a finger at the bald young man and screamed.

Grinning, the bald man reached under his coat, stalking toward the literary agent. Selma's face was so paralyzed from all the Botox injections, it couldn't betray a single recognizable emotion in the terrible moment.

Others began to scream. Ace yelled for the children to cover their eyes and hit the floor.

The stranger snarled, "Reject *this*, you old whore!"

He got off a single trigger pull before Ace's shot exploded the gunman's head.

In the moment, Ace blessed again his rare, city-granted Concealed Carry permit. Then he looked to Selma, who was wide-eyed and shaking.

Lucky Hyena: the shooter's gun had jammed or something. Otherwise, the stranger would have killed her with his single, point-blank shot.

Satisfied she was okay, and the gunman was indeed dead, Santa-Ace thrust his gun back in his boot. The barrel burned his ankle, a little. He looked around the literary office.

All those kids were going to need therapy: Santa would never loom the same way for them again. And some of their grateful, MILFy mothers, bless them, one and all, looked ready to lay the strapping, gun-toting Santa in a NYC minute.

They were seated in Selma's office, draining drinks and talking it through. The party had immediately fallen apart, of course.

The cops were at last gone. The shooter's body had been carried off and was being cut open somewhere by now.

The killer was some loudly defrocked lit blogger with writing aspirations of his own. His career as a critic had scorched out recently in a Web-wide "flame war" that correctly outed the blogger as a no-talent nihilist with a particular disdain for literary women.

Sufficient evidence had been turned up in a cursory search of his apartment to definitively link Joe Chandler to the killings of the two literary agents. Selma would have been his third victim if extreme wear to its firing pin hadn't rendered his weapon defective.

Again, *lucky Selma*. She drained another drink and said, "Well, at least it's all over. You *will* see me home tonight, after all this, won't you?"

Ace, back in familiar and tailored street clothes, said, "Whatever the circumstances, it's been good to talk like this, quiet and for a while, just the two of us. Been too long. Frankly, I was getting the feeling lately you might be working up to severing our business relationship."

Selma's still face managed to look slightly uncomfortable. Her eyes hinted at maybe having been found out. Certainly, The Hyena appeared caught off-guard. She said, "Hold that thought, lover. All this excitement and booze—I need to pee *soo* wicked bad. Back in a flash."

*Right*. So it *was* like that. She was really off to think of some way to put it to him.

He cursed... looked at her desk. A stack of books lay there. Near the top of the pile was one of his scant nonfiction books, a how-to for fiction writers about guns and other weapons. Pantywaist authors were forever screwing up when writing about handguns, particularly, wrongly putting silencers on revolvers and stupid mistakes like that. His book had been intended to remedy such rookie writing errors.

He picked up Selma's copy of *Don't Shoot Yourself in the Foot* and saw that it was actually bookmarked.

Still seething, despite himself, Ace checked to see what Selma had tagged in his book.

*Well, well...*

This terrible epiphany ensued that put a *very broad smile* on his face.

Selma had been researching ways to sabotage firearms.

She found him sitting in her chair, his feet crossed on her desk. She said, "What the hell do you think you're doing, mister?"

"Just trying it out," Ace said, still smiling. "Maybe I could learn to love sitting on this side of the desk."

His insolence seemed to set her on her long-ago determined course. She said hatefully, "Well, stop trying it out, and I guess, awkward as it is to say after what you just did for me, you're right, Ace. Frankly, the men's book market has changed, and it's *not* going to change back. The male audience for your books is literally dying off and *fast*. So as you apparently intuited, I have decided that you and I can no longer continue as—"

Ace held up a big hand. He had his gun at the ready, out of sight in case things went south, but he didn't expect that to happen, not really. He said, "No, sugar. Let me tell *you* how things stand between us."

Over two tense and profanity-laced hours, they talked it through. Then they worked it all out.

When they were done, they had forged their new, shared *professional* future.

Ace set the terms. What else could she do? He had Selma by the short hair, after all. He'd correctly deduced most if it before she grudgingly confirmed his audacious logical leaps.

The publishing industry was circling the drain, slowly but surely. That came as no news, of course. Contracts were drying up; agencies were shrinking. Fewer and fewer of even the A-List authors were reliable sellers of late.

Selma confirmed she'd inherited her recently dead competitor agents' stables, almost to a man and a woman. At the very least, it bought her more time, desperately needed liquidity.

She'd conned insane and woman-hating Joe Chandler into doing her bloody bidding; this crazy pitch that he'd walk on an insanity plea to be followed by a Hyena-orchestrated book and movie contract that would set him on his way, at last. The final scheme had called for his gun to misfire, and for Joe to fall to his knees, crying and asking where he was… who were these people. Why did he have this gun in his hand…

That's the sorry scene Joe thought he was going to play this bloody night.

But after Joe had done the deadly deed for her twice, Selma had arranged for the unstable lit blogger to meet his own demise at Ace's steady and sure hand. Selma had decided to do that before Joe could go publicly berserk again—before he could even rat out The Hyena.

Talk about publish or perish: Ace couldn't believe the stone-faced literary agent's coldblooded, cut-throat scheming.

So Ace set these new terms: The Hyena had no choice but to meet them. The Iron Seal ended up with a no-cut representation contract that only he could sever and a tidy percentage of Selma's newly engorged literary agency.

Also, he walked away with a recorded, full confession to her crimes that would keep him safely out of reach of The Hyena's lethal plotting skills and safe from her vengeful impulses.

As he stood and pocketed his new contract and allied agency profit-sharing agreement, Ace gave Selma a last hard look. She hesitated, as if she wanted something else from him.

Finally, she said, "You're not just *leaving* me here tonight after all this, are you? We're kindred, you must see that now. I simply cannot be alone in my present state; can't be alone with my thoughts. Ace, it's the holidays after all, and my conscience is so, well, you know…"

Of course, he did, and it set Ace's head spinning.

Despite all their new agreements and his self-insuring evidence against her, he actually feared this woman. He feared Selma, at least until he could get all this precious paper notarized, get his iPhone recording onto a recordable disc and into some safe deposit box or two, maybe even three, at least one of them off-shore for added insurance.

Ace said, "I don't rule out anything between us, not down the road, Selma. Not even that horizontal business. But you asked earlier if I had plans for *this* night. You know that little blonde you hired to play female elf, the one in the green velveteen jumper? Turns out, she's a recently retired porn starlet whose body of work I know and quite admire. We clicked over drinks before the shooting started. I'm headed her way now."

He tried to think of some exit line, some last thing to say as he made this famous final exit. He saw a stray sprig of mistletoe dangling over her door. Ace reached up, plucked it free. Gun in hand, he walked over and held the mistletoe over their heads. He kissed Selma's cold, ivory cheek, gun in his coat pocket, pointed at her heart.

Her eyes wished him dead.

Smiling, Ace cuffed her chin and said, "Have yourself a merry little Christmas, baby."

# FELIZ NAVIDAD

## Sam Hawken

### Author's note

In mid-2014 a wave of undocumented migrants swamped the United States' southern border. Most of them were under the age of eighteen and many were as young as six or seven years old, all traveling without adults to accompany them. They came from all across Central America, fleeing the scourge of violence American demand for illegal drugs has created. These children believed that if they turned themselves into the American authorities, they would have a chance at a new life free from danger.

The massive surge of youths has abated somewhat, but the journey north continues for many thousands desperate for safety and opportunity. This is the story of one such child.

—Sam Hawken, author of *La Frontera*

---

O n the day Raúl Navarro left San Pedro Sula in Honduras, his older brother, Osvaldo, was killed in the street. They didn't know if he was shot deliberately, or if he had simply been unlucky enough to be on the scene. Two others died in the same incident. Raúl packed his things in a blue Adidas gym bag, said goodbye to his mother and younger brother and went out of the apartment and down the stairs. He had he had five hundred and eleven dollars in American cash in his pocket, everything his family had been able to put together. He was fourteen years old.

He took a bus to the city limits, riding until there were no more stops to be made. He was the last person on the bus besides an old man with a ratty paperback book with no cover. Raúl helped the old man get off at the end of the line, then turned south and walked.

It took him the better part of two hours to reach Chamelecón at the southeast corner of the El Merendón National Forest, and he was feeling good about the journey. He stopped only for a bottle of water at a vendor selling from a cart. He kept on, walking along the CA-4 highway. It started to rain.

He walked for the rest of the day, and when it grew dark he stepped back into the forest out of sight of the road and lay down under the spreading branches of a pine tree, his bed a thick layer of old needles. This kept the worst of the rain from him, and the ground was not soaked. It was cooler than it had been during the day, but it only dropped into the twenties. He was warm enough in his fleece running jacket and jeans, though he woke up with dew forming on his body.

Things went on like this for three days until he made the border with Guatemala. He was ragged by then and his clothes were dirty. The men at the border crossing looked at him suspiciously, but he tried to smile when he lied to them about where he was going and what he would do when he got there. He knew it was another three or four days' walk to Guatemala City and already his feet hurt and his legs were very tired. It was only the beginning. They ignored the fact that he was only fourteen and let him through.

Raúl was careful with his money and he didn't eat on opposite days, and then only a little. He knew it robbed him of energy, but he only had a small amount of cash to make the journey and he could not afford to spend much. On a bad day he was forced to drink from a puddle of rainwater formed in a depression in the road. He kept wearing the same clothes he left wearing until he was close to the Mexican border, and he only changed when he was within sight of the crossing, ducking between two buildings and shucking off his filthy garments to replace them with fresher ones.

"Where are you from?" the Mexican at the crossing asked him.

"Honduras."

"I'm not stupid," the Mexican said. "You have a Honduran passport. *Where* in Honduras?"

"San Pedro Sula."

The Mexican exchanged glances with the uniformed man nearest him, then looked back to Raúl. "And you've come to Mexico to visit your Mexican relatives."

"No, I—"

"Mexican relatives," the man said firmly, cutting Raúl off. "Did you say they were in Oaxaca?"

"I didn't say anything."

"Oaxaca," the Mexican said, and he stamped Raul's passport. "Your mother is coming up in line?"

"Um… yes."

"Good, because I cannot let a minor across the border without an adult escort."

The Mexican gave Raúl his passport still open. The ink from the stamp was fresh and dark. "Thank you, sir," Raúl said.

"Don't thank me. Move along."

Raúl moved along. He crossed with a collection of adults and children he didn't know and took up alongside the highway as he had all the way from his home. The numbers had changed, but the road was just the same: two lanes heading in either direction, the middle lines nearly invisible from sun and rain.

He forgot what day it was. All there was for him was walking and restless sleep in doorways and alleys and out in the wilds between towns. He followed the signs north through Chiapas, aware only that he was moving forward step by step and that eventually the journey would come to an end. When he reached Tuxtla Gutiérrez he spotted a date on a calendar in a small shop where he bought a sweet bun and a carton of milk.

He had been on the road for two weeks. He was unclean down to the pores and his skin itched all the time. He found a public washroom and waited until there was a lull, then he stripped to the waist and washed himself in the sink, using a dirty shirt as a washcloth. There was only powdered soap in the dispenser and it was gritty against his body, but when he was done he did not smell so bad and even his hair had lost some of its greasiness.

Ten days to Oaxaca, the city where the Mexican pretended he had family. Nine days to Mexico City. More than two weeks to walk the distance to Monterrey and then four more days to reach Reynosa on the Rio Grande across from McAllen, Texas. He dragged into Reynosa with numb feet, feeling drained in every way. His clothes fit loosely on him because he had lost much weight on the journey. He had run out of clean clothes a long time before and hadn't wanted to spare the cash to clean them at a lavandería. Now he saw the river beyond a metal fence with many holes in it and on the far side America.

He didn't wait. He pushed his bag through a hole in the fence and then squeezed through after it, tearing his shirt. The embankment was steep, but he crashed down to the water and plunged in. It was colder than he expected.

The current was strong, though the surface seemed placid. He tried to swim while holding the Adidas bag, but he couldn't. It was gone in an instant. He heard shouting in English from the far bank. He stroked with his arm and kicked with his legs. He wished he'd left his shoes behind.

In the middle of the crossing he managed to look up on the far side and he saw men in uniform and a white truck with a green stripe. The men had something round and orange and they climbed down their side of the river, which was reinforced with concrete. They threw the orange ring into the water and it landed a distance to Raul's right. He struck out toward it, brushed it with his fingers, got a grip he would not release. He put his other hand on the ring and hung on as they hauled him in.

The men grabbed him under his arms when he reached the American bank, hauling him dripping from the water. One of them was speaking Spanish to him, but he didn't understand because his head was whirling. They laid him down on the dirt. Raúl struggled to focus on the man who spoke.

"You could have died!" the man said in Spanish. "You could have died!"

Raúl reached for the man's arm and caught it and squeezed. "I am not dead," he said. "I am in America."

An ambulance came. An overweight medic examined him with his shirt off, and Raúl knew the Border Patrol officers watching him were talking about how thin he was. When the examination was over, he wrapped up in a plastic thing like a blanket, only it looked like tinfoil. It kept him warm all the way to the hospital.

At the hospital he was stripped completely out of his wet clothes and given soft footies with rubber strips on the soles, and two gowns he could wear front and back to cover himself. He lay on a comfortable bed in a room with a television playing an English-language station, and an orderly brought him food, real food. It took all his willpower not shove the sandwich into his face with both hands, or to slurp the Jell-O out of its container. He consumed a whole banana in two bites. The milk he got in a paper carton was guzzled down in a second. After a while, the orderly came back to him and asked him a question in English. "*No hablo Inglés*," Raúl told the man, and the orderly went away.

Eventually he saw a doctor, who took his vital signs and asked him in Spanish to do things like breathe deeply and say *ah*. "Have you been sick recently? A cold or anything?" the doctor asked him.

"Not sick. Very hungry."

"I'll see about getting you some more food," the doctor said. He was dark-skinned and Latino, and the name on his hospital identification was Garcia. "And then they'll want to take you."

"Take me where?"

"Somewhere you can rest and sleep."

"Can't I stay here for a while?"

Dr. Garcia looked at Raúl with sad eyes. "I'm afraid not. This is a hospital, not a shelter. Don't worry. It will be all right."

The same orderly as before brought Raúl a fresh tray of food. He ate in a more measured fashion this time. By the time he was done he felt almost full.

It was an hour before men in uniform arrived. Raúl didn't recognize their badges or their faces, but they were authority, and that was all that mattered. They brought him clothes: white socks and underpants and a t-shirt, white slip-on shoes and then loose pants and a top made of bright orange linen. "Put these on," said one of them. "Don't take too long."

Raúl reluctantly shed the hospital gowns and got into the clothes. It was prisoners' clothing, though it lacked any writing to indicate where the wearer belongs. When was finished dressing he said, "I'm ready," and the uniformed men re-entered the room. One of them put handcuffs on him, though they cuffed his hands in front.

He was led out of the hospital past many faces, white, black and brown. They watched him with a mixture of emotions, though most seemed sad for him. Others looked strangely, inexplicably angry, including a white man who flushed red when Raúl marched by. The man whispered something to the woman with him and the both of them glared at Raúl until he was out of sight.

The uniformed men put Raúl in a white van and they drove for a while. He could not be certain how long. They were in McAllen properly now, not just in the part that skirted the river. Everywhere there were unreadable signs in English and cars and activity. Spanish appeared regularly as if to comfort him, offering drugstores and televisions and places to cash checks. Though it was not so terribly different from what he saw in Reynosa, it was also alien. These things he saw were *American* and he was not in his home or the home of anyone south of the river.

They approached a forbidding, angular building made of red and gray stone. The van cruised past a line of police units on the way to a gated entrance manned by another uniform.

The van drove down an angled slope into an underground receiving area where finally the driver killed the engine and Raúl's escorts got out.

He was released from the back of the van and brought through two sets of doors with electric locks into a room with a long counter divided into sections. People were at every section, speaking in Spanish or a mixture of Spanish and English to the men and women in uniform behind the counter. All the people doing the talking were cuffed like Raúl.

"Wait behind the blue line," said one of the men with Raúl. The other one left. Raúl stood behind the blue line.

It took most of an hour before someone at the counter could see him. Raúl listened as his escort talked to the woman in his section in English. They both laughed and then finally Raúl was alone with the woman. A man on his left spoke animatedly in Salvadoran-accented Spanish. On his right, a Mexican woman was barely audible through the tears she shed.

"My name is Agent Flores," said the woman behind the counter. "What is your name?"

"Raúl Navarro."

Agent Flores typed. Raúl could not see the screen. "Where are you from, Raúl?"

"San Pedro Sula. In Honduras."

She looked directly at him. "How old are you, Raúl?"

"Fourteen."

"Where are your parents?"

"My father is in prison. My mother is at home."

"You came alone?"

"Yes."

"Why?"

Raúl hesitated. "They say… they say if a boy comes here, he can stay. That they won't send him away. Is that true?"

"Sometimes," Agent Flores said, and Raúl thought she looked sad. His eyes strayed past her to the Christmas decorations on the wall. Santa Claus and snowmen and mistletoe and holly. And Christmas trees and snowflakes.

She asked him other questions, about how many brothers and sisters he had, and where he had gone on his long walk. She asked him how much they said he weighed at the hospital and how tall he was. She asked him if he had relatives in the United States. She asked him question after question for a long time until finally there were no more questions.

"What happens to me now?" Raúl asked.

Agent Flores smiled unhappily. "They'll take you somewhere to stay."

The building was full of many halls and doors. Someone new took Raúl up an elevator to a high floor and brought him out into a concrete hallway ringing with the sound of children's voices. It sounded like a school before the first bell rang, high laughter and shouted jokes and cursing and the rush of a hundred simultaneous conversations. After a short stretch of hallway the interior of the building opened up and there were bars on both sides.

The teenagers were broken into two groups, boys on one side and girls on the other. There were a two hundred or more in each holding area and many of the tinfoil-looking blankets. Rubber sleeping mats lay haphazardly all over the floor, being trodden on by kids in sneakers and in white slip-ons like Raúl's. The boys closest to the bars were yelling to the girls, trying to get their attention, and some of the girls were yelling back, not always friendly. Raúl tried to keep his eyes straight ahead.

He was turned toward a door and the door was opened with a heavy brass key. The man who escorted him said, "Look at me."

Raúl looked at the man. He was tall and straight and heavy in the chest and shoulders like a man used to lifting weights. His hair was shot through with grey. "Yes, *señor*?" Raúl asked.

"No '*señor*.' It's *mister*. I am Mr. Martinez. I'm in charge of this floor. If you have questions, you ask to speak with me. If you have problems, you come to me. If you have a need, I'm the one you look for. Do you understand? *Mister* Martinez?"

"Yes, Mr. Martinez."

"Good. And don't let any of these little bastards give you any shit. Later someone will bring you a mat for sleeping and a blanket. You'll be all right until then."

"Yes, Mr. Martinez."

"Go."

Raúl went. He let Mr. Martinez lock the door behind him and he faced the pandemonium of the holding area. There were a few tables made of stainless steel and bolted to the floor, along with their seating, but they were overrun with boys. None of the boys he saw seemed younger than thirteen, but some were clearly close to eighteen or over it. There were angry looks and curious looks and looks of complete indifference.

All at once the looks turned into talking and Raúl was asked a dozen questions at once. Where he was from, what he was doing here, did they say anything about letting anyone out, would they bring extra food for dinner, how old was he, was he going to a family in the States, and on and on and on.

He tried to answer all the questions as well as he could, but there were too many to keep track of, and very soon the eager questions stopped, and he was back to being ignored. Raúl worked his way through the crowd along the bars, settling into a spot where the corner met the cage, and sat down. He put a hand on a bar and felt the cold metal under the mint-green paint. For the first time since he left home, he felt like crying. The voices pummeled him endlessly.

Every half an hour or so, a man in uniform came by to check on them. Raúl also noticed cameras in the ceiling, protected inside plastic bubbles, looking down on them all. He imagined Mr. Martinez keeping an eye on him in his corner, alone among a multitude, and telling the other men in uniform that this kid was all right. Decent and respectful. They taught them well in Honduras. Not like those Salvadoran kids.

His eyelids drooped despite himself and he drifted into a sort of half-sleep. The roar of the voices, echoing and re-echoing off the flat concrete, reduced to a background tumult and there were images of soft beds and his room and trays of food, each more delicious than the last.

Raúl wasn't sure how long he drifted this way, but eventually he opened his eyes again and nothing had changed. He felt a pressure in his bowels and he stood up, looking for a place to go. He saw the word RESTROOM emblazoned above an open doorway, and under it the word BAÑO. Little by little, he worked his way through the crowd until he could get there.

With each step closer to the restroom he could smell the growing stench of urine and feces. By the time he was at the door, the odor was almost overwhelming. He stepped over the threshold, and his clean white shoe splashed in a shallow pool of water. He saw the whole interior of the restroom was flooded to the depth of a centimeter, and the water was not clean. Chunks of raw excrement lay on the floor, some swathed in toilet tissue that had soaked through.

He went to the stalls to find a toilet and discovered the first one was so full of waste that it had mounded up over the seat and begun to spill down the sides. The next one was the same and the next and the next. Some of the boys had even taken to moving their bowels into the urinals along one wall, so that half of them were clotted with stools.

The pressure was too much to ignore. The food from the hospital had worked through him rapidly. He stepped into one of the stalls and took down his pants and his underpants, only he could not let them fall to his ankles lest they soak in the filthy water. Nor could he sit on the seat because of the accumulated filth. Instead he half-bent and half-squatted over the clogged toilet and did what he had to do. When he was done, he used what little toilet tissue was left in the dispenser to clean himself.

He washed his hands in a sink and fled the restroom as soon as he was able. When he returned to his spot by the bars and sat down, he did cry, though he hid his face and made no sound.

Food time was a time of chaos, as the dozens pressed up against the one open door, trying to grab a meal before anyone else could. They were given small paper bags with a cold sandwich and a bag of chips inside and a small container of apple juice. Eventually, all the mob were sorted out, but for a long time Raúl thought he would not get any food at all.

He ate in his corner and ignored the sound of chewing and intermittent squabbling over who had rights to what bit of a meal exchange. The sandwich was tasteless, the bread soaked in something that was not mayonnaise. Raúl ate it anyway, because he knew without asking that to leave any food uneaten in this place was to lose it forever.

From time to time he looked out through the bars at the girls in the opposite holding area. They were much the same as the boys, sparking up into screaming matches that burned out as quickly as they started. He saw a girl sitting near the bars almost directly across from him, her back to the others, looking out at Raúl while she ate and he ate. She raised a hand to him in a half-wave and he waved back. They said nothing to each other.

After the meal there was a collection of the garbage, and once again the single door was mobbed. Once two teens broke out into the passageway and tried to run, but Mr. Martinez and the other uniformed men put them quickly back in place. Raúl did not try to escape. He did not know where he would go even if he were to slip out of the holding area, out of the building and onto the street. The entire plan had been to make the crossing and surrender to the first American in a uniform he could find. That was done, though this was not the result he had been led to expect.

Raúl held off using the restroom as long as he possibly could, but finally he was forced into the mire to urinate. He would rather have died than face the toilets again. He huddled up in his spot, gently rocking himself. The girl was still there, glancing up at him from time to time, but not staring.

He heard her voice for the first time a little while later on. "*Oye,*" he heard her say. "Hey. Hey, you!"

He looked. "What do you want?"

"What's your name?"

"Raúl."

"I am Beatriz."

"Okay."

"How old are, Raúl?"

"How old are *you*?"

"Fourteen."

Raúl straightened a little. "I'm also fourteen."

"Where are you from?"

"Honduras."

"I'm from Mexico. Do you know a place called Xalapa?"

Raúl thought about it, and shook his head. "I've never heard of it."

"It's a city. Do you come from the city or the country?"

"The city. San Pedro Sula."

"Where is that?"

"I said it's in Honduras."

Beatriz made a sour face. "If you're going to be rude, then I won't talk to you."

"I'm sorry."

Footsteps sounded in the passageway, and Beatriz suddenly became very interested in her lap. Raúl strained to see farther down the hall, but he could not see who was coming until they were nearly upon him. He recognized Mr. Martinez, and saw that the man carried a rolled up foam mat and a folded blanket like all the tinfoil-looking blankets in the holding area.

Martinez spotted Raúl and pointed toward the door. "You," he said, "meet me over there."

Raúl hurried to get to the door, stepping over and around the densely packed crowd. Mr. Martinez opened the door, but there was no rush to escape this time. The other boys fell back instead, and Raúl stood alone at the threshold with the man.

"These are yours," Mr. Martinez told Raúl, and he thrust the bedding into Raúl's hands.

"Thank you."

"I read through your documents and it says your brother was killed not long ago."

"Yes, Mr. Martinez."

"You have another brother, though."

"Yes. He is eleven."

"It's good that he isn't here. It's almost Christmas. He should be with his family. Like you should. This is no place for a boy. Not for any of you. Why would you come here and put yourself through this?"

Raúl shook his head slowly. "In my country there is so much killing. The gangs control everything. What they can't take, they destroy. The people who won't follow them, they murder. Someone has to get out and tell Americans what is happening. So my mother and my brother can come here and be safe."

Mr. Martinez looked down at him. "Your mother and your brother are never coming here."

He closed the door and walked away. The level of conversation picked up around Raúl, and the circle closed. Soon it was as if the man had not been there at all. Raúl retreated to his spot.

Beatriz was watching him. "Your brother died?" she asked.

"Yes."

"That's terrible. My uncle was killed by the *narcos*. It's everywhere."

"Not here."

"No," Beatriz agreed. "Not here."

They had nothing else to say to each other after that, and soon it was time for lights out. One of Mr. Martinez's men came through yelling in Spanish for everyone to lie down and go to sleep. Half the overhead illumination was shut down so it was not truly dark. Raúl found he could not unroll his mat entirely in his place, nor could he unwind his body to lie full length. He was forced into a curled position, almost hugging his knees, with the papery blanket over him for warmth.

Despite himself, he drifted. In his dream-state he heard Beatriz whispering to him. Then he realized it was not a dream at all, but her urgent whisper through the bars and across the space that separated them. "Hey," she said. "Hey, Raúl!"

"It's time to sleep," Raúl hissed back.

"In a week it will be Christmas. Good things happen at Christmas."

Raúl only nodded, and then he went back to sleep.

Each day it was the same. Food came three times a day, sandwiches for lunch and dinner and a sticky roll and milk for breakfast. Every other day they were taken out in shifts to use showers. They were locked into the stalls alone and given five minutes to clean themselves. The toilets were mucked out once, but soon were clogged with filth, and the process started all over again.

Talk began to spread among the teenagers on this level, both on the girls' side and the boys', that something special was set to happen on Christmas Day. Beatriz was the one who first told Raúl this, and one of the boys near him overheard them talking. The rumor spread rapidly. Soon everyone demanded of the uniformed men and women who looked after the floor what was going to happen. They were told to sit and be quiet and mind their own business.

Some of the boys and girls were taken away and did not come back. This fueled the speculation even more. But then new boys and girls were brought in to take their places. The holding areas were jammed head to toe, and there was barely enough space to form a thought. Raúl held onto his station and refused to be budged.

Mr. Martinez came once a day to look in on them, and he took time to speak with Raúl at his place by the bars. He knew many of the other boys by name, but Raúl felt especially singled out whenever Mr. Martinez spoke to him. He did not like talking to the other boys, and Beatriz could not talk to him all the time, so Mr. Martinez was the best of all possible worlds.

"It's Christmas tomorrow," Mr. Martinez told Raúl one day.

"I know. There is a lot of talking about—"

"I know what they're talking about. They've been on about it all week. Don't listen to them."

"But something must happen on Christmas," Raúl insisted.

"Maybe something will," Mr. Martinez said. "We'll see."

And that was the end of their conversation. The day before Christmas went on the way every other day had, with talk and jokes and fights and shouting and singing and chaos. Raúl kept himself to himself and didn't speak even to Beatriz.

There was night and then it was Christmas day. The lights came on and the holding areas awoke with stretching and yawns. Raúl struggled to bring some life into his stiff limbs. Every night he spent curled up was harder than the night before. His joints ached. He felt old. Lines formed for the restroom and the reek of urine was everywhere.

Breakfast did not come on time and there were rumblings. After an hour's delay there was anger in the air.

Raúl heard the sleigh bells first, and then the jolly sound of someone booming, "Ho, ho, ho!" There were many footfalls in the passage. And then there he was: Mr. Martinez in a red suit with white trim, a floppy cap with a puffball on the point draped over his skull. He was followed by the morning crew with the breakfast carts.

A loud and rousing cheer rose from the boys' side of the floor, and then a higher-pitched response from the girls. Soon the doors were open and food was dispensed. Mr. Martinez kept chortling away and the bags were all distributed. Inside, along with the usual milk and roll, was a piece of wrapped chocolate and an orange. Soon the smell of orange zest was in the air instead of the earthy stink of the restroom and the closely packed bodies.

Raúl ate and was happy and saw Beatriz smiling at him as she sectioned her orange. There was more laughter and less shouting now than there had been on days before. Raúl felt light.

It was close to lunchtime when Mr. Martinez returned without his Santa suit. He came with another uniformed man, and they opened the door to the boys' holding area. "Raúl!" Mr. Martinez called. "Raul! Honduras! Come on! Bring everything!"

Raúl gathered up his things and hurried to the door. He hadn't yet unwrapped and eaten his chocolate yet. "I am here," he said.

Mr. Martinez smiled at him. "Come with us."

They took him down from the high floor to another place with many rooms and offices. He was put in a new cell, much smaller, all alone. A little while later a woman brought him a large paper sack. In the sack were the clothes he'd worn the day he'd crossed the border. "Put those on," the woman said. "They've been cleaned."

He stripped off the orange suit, but he kept the socks and the underpants and the undershirt even though he was sure they wanted him to take those off, too. He changed into his old clothes and waited. After a long while someone else came to get him, and he was brought through to another holding area, still fairly small, where he was held with three boys who were very young.

Mr. Martinez came to them after a while. "This is the end of your time with us, Raúl," he said.

"Is it time?" Raúl asked. "Have they decided to let me stay?"

"Your case was reviewed by a judge. His decision was to let you go. There's a plane leaving the airport in three hours. You'll be on it."

Raúl's vision blurred. He felt tears and wiped at them. "I can't go back to Honduras! I can't! I came so far!"

"I know," Mr. Martinez said somberly. "I'm sorry."

The other boys were crying, too. They had only a few things between them and soon they were all picked up by men in uniforms and put in a van and taken to the airport. They were given seats on the tightly packed planes, and a man with a badge, but no uniform, flew with them. The flight to Honduras took five hours. There was time to reach home for Christmas dinner.

On the day Raúl Navarro left San Pedro Sula again, his cousin, Emilio, was killed in a clash over drug territory. Raúl packed his things in a pale green pillowcase with clouds printed on it, said goodbye to his mother and younger brother, and went out of the apartment and down the stairs. He had one hundred three dollars in American cash in his pocket, everything he had left from his sojourn north. He was fourteen years old.

# CHERRY PINK AND APPLE BLOSSOM WHITE

## David Hogan

David Hogan is an acclaimed playwright whose works have been widely produced and the author of *The Last Island*, a universal tale of escape, love and redemption set on a Greek island.
"Hogan's adept storytelling makes us ponder our spiritual essence."

*—The Greek Star*

---

The cards fall in perfect order: king, queen, jack… diamonds first, followed by hearts, clubs, and spades. His hands are steady, surprisingly so, as he flips the top one from the deck. Even now, his hands are skilled; even now, with the arthritic fingers bent in odd directions and the subtle quiver, his hands don't betray him. His hands remember. He inspects each card before placing it down, leaning forward to within inches of its face. Sometimes, when he realizes that the card he is looking at is precisely the needed card, there will be, in his abandoned eyes, a spark. And in that spark, her lost father

re-emerges, awash in the cross currents of time and conscious-
ness and wonder.

It's because of this spark that Mary called her brother,
Brendan, back to Boston just before Christmas when he'd
have preferred to be with his own family. It's because of
this spark that Brendan is now gathering leaves on this grey
and bitter December morning. Today will be their final gift
as children, a Christmas gift of sorts, and there will be the
leaves and an unknown woman and water and a window.

Mary looks out at the park across the street. She played tag
and hide-and-seek in that park and kissed her first boy behind
the big tree in the corner. He'd been a curly headed boy named
Patrick, and they missed the first time they tried, his lips landing on the bridge of her nose. But Mary was a stubborn sort
and she let him try again, having committed this far, feeling
she'd gone past a point, and there was no sense in turning back
no matter how bad Patrick's aim was. He connected with her
chin on the second attempt, but on the third he was successful. She was eleven, and when their lips met, soft and wet, she
sprinted back to the house where she was now standing with
her father playing Solitaire behind her.

"Dad," she says. "I have to talk to you."

But she doesn't. Not really. Even if he acknowledges her
presence, or calls her by her late mother's name – who passed
peacefully four years ago – there will be no discussion, no
explanation, no consent. He's past that. She would like to talk
to him about what she intends to do tomorrow. To lend him
some residual dignity. But age – it wounds, confiscates, and
undermines, and dignity must be re-defined. Her father's eyes
resemble tunnels, dark with forfeitures he's no longer aware
of. Once again, Mary weighs the value of responsibility, the

cost of guilt. Considers how love is the tilted scale on which they are appraised.

"Mary. Mary, can I talk to you?"

It's as if she actually hears him say the words, as if he is once again the man with bushy, black eyebrows that she knew when he was driving her to college for her first year. Her eighteen year old heart had been broken that summer, and Mary had refused herself the usual teen-age consolations of music and verse and alcohol. She spent hours each day motionless on her bed, wallowing monastically in her heartache. Determined. Stubborn. She didn't want sympathy. What she wanted was to work through it, understand it and subdue it.

Her parents seemed to understand and, by the end of that summer, as she rode in the car with her father on her way to college, the subject of her break-up had never been mentioned. She turned on the car radio to avoid a last chance at such a conversation. Turned it to a news station that she thought her father might enjoy. She smiled and looked out the side window thinking she just might escape, that the issue would never have to be addressed. But when they entered the Mass Pike, her father turned off the radio, and her heart sank. This is it, she thought, the discussion I've spent three months avoiding.

"Can I tell you a story?" he said.

"Sure," she said. Her father wasn't one to tell stories, and Mary wondered how long he'd been rehearsing this one. She expected a story about his break-up with some 'sweet gal' who was a 'great dancer', and how badly he'd been hurt, but that if he hadn't gone through that he'd never have met her mother and she might never have been born. Something along those lines. Mary was thankful that it was a story though, and that she could sit and listen and not have to engage.

"Thanks," her father said, as if he knew it was a burden for her to listen. "So yeah, one day just after I'd started college, like you're about to do, I was walking to campus in Chestnut Hill. Now, I was older than most of the students, having fought in the war." He turned to her. "The Korean War."

"I know what war, Dad."

"I suppose you do. Now, I had a little bit of money, and I can remember clinking the coins against each other in my pocket. I always liked that sound. And the wind was blowing, and the day was kind of damp and cold. And there were wet leaves on the ground, and maybe they were rotting or something, I don't know. But they had a peculiar smell."

She sighed, too loudly, wondering if she was going to have to listen to him describe the weather for the next two hours. Maybe that's why he never told stories, she thought.

Her father laughed, unoffended. "Give me a chance, Mary."

"Sorry, Dad."

"I'm going on, I know," he said. "But it seems important, you know, the leaves, the smell, the cold, all that. Because just before I got to campus, I walked past this open window, and there was this girl's bare leg hanging out of it. There was loud music inside her room, and I can still remember the song, *Cherry Pink and Apple Blossom White*. Don't know where they got that title. Where do they get song titles from?"

"I don't know, Dad." She spoke to the window.

"Doesn't matter. So, you know, I was walking by that window and saw this girl's leg, and I just stopped. I can remember it like it was yesterday, me standing there wondering why this girl's pretty bare leg was swinging there. Was it for me? Did she know me? It was so cold, and it didn't seem to make sense. You didn't see a lot of bare legs in my day. Not in winter and never hanging out a window. It was just hanging there, so easy, so free and – now I hope you don't mind your old man saying – even sexy. And right then, right then, Mary, I realized that I could do anything in the world. I could talk to this girl and ask her why her leg was hanging out of the window and would she like to go to a movie. Or I could tug on her foot and pull her into my arms. I was on my way to college, college for God's sake – I didn't think I'd ever go to college – and I could study anything in the world, science or religion or history. Or I could run away and join the Merchant Marines. There were no adults around and no more missions or orders to follow. Nothing. I had a little money in my pocket, and there was nothing in the world but this girl's leg and just... possibility. Right then, the whole world was just possibility. I'm not sure I've ever felt that way again.

"So that's it, Mary. That's all I have to say. I've thought of that moment many times since then, and it's my hope, now that you're going to college and will be on your own, that you have some moments like that. You've had a tough summer, and I just want you to try and have as many moments like that as you can. Can you promise me that? Mary? Just that?"

She continued staring out the window, away from her father, afraid to turn back, afraid to let him see how he'd gotten to her, that this was perhaps what she needed to hear, the sort of wisdom she'd been looking to find all summer. She wiped away the tears with her sleeve, hoping her father wouldn't notice. If he did, he didn't mention it, merely turned the radio back on.

As far as Mary can recall, that's the only story her father ever told – her one-story father who's just now finishing another game of Solitaire and coming to what is, for Mary, the astonishing part. Because somehow her father knows to scoop up the cards in reverse order, row by row, ace to king, spades first, then the clubs, the hearts, the diamonds, the sequence never varying, so that when he lays them out again, they'll be in the right order. The cards will be perfect again. And she wonders how, in the chaos of his mind and memory, he knows how to do such a thing, wonders what determines the things that go or remain.

Brendan walks in the door stomping dirt from the bottom of his boots. When their father became ill, Mary and Brendan made an arrangement. She would leave her job as a news producer for a local television station and move back home, and Brendan, who made good money working for a bank in Charlotte, would pay the bills. It'd worked for both of them. Until recently. Until she could no longer provide the care her father required and asked Brendan to return home before Christmas.

"Let's do it," he says now from the doorway.

Half an hour later, Mary is in the back seat of Brendan's rent-a-car with her father clothed in layers and tightly strapped next to her. She has a bottle of water in her pocket and they are all headed to Chestnut Hill, on the west side of Boston, where her father attended college. He'd resisted when they pulled him away from the card game and made it clear by going rigid that he wanted to stay. Mary wondered if they weren't being cruel. The cards might be enough for him, perfect game after perfect game, each one as extraordinary as the one before.

Her father is mute during the trip, his head bobbing slightly as they drive down the road. This will be their last trip as a family, and Mary thinks it fitting that it's being taken on this road, Route 9, which had been the central corridor of their lives for so long. She looks at the back of Brendan's head, his hair just beginning to thin. He'd been the wilder of the two children, often getting into trouble for drinking and staying out too late. He didn't drink anymore and was the father of twins, a boy and girl, who were sophomores in a large Charlotte high school.

"Do you let your kids go to parties?" she asks.

Brendan catches her eyes in the rear view mirror and smiles. "No. No drinking, no dates, no parties, no late nights."

"What do you say when they ask you what you did?"

"I lie, Mary. Flat out, I lie." He thinks about this for a moment. "It's funny. First, you lie to your parents, then you lie to your kids."

You don't have to lie to Dad anymore, Mary thinks, but she doesn't say it. She doesn't know how to say it in a way that doesn't sound offensive to one or the other of them. She doesn't want it to sound offensive. She wants it to sound true, which is what it is, but she's not sure how to do that and so says nothing. They arrive in Chestnut Hill and park on the side of a two-lane residential street.

"Give me a minute," Brendan says.

He walks down the street and enters the screened-in porch of a brown two story house.

"You okay, Dad?" Mary asks her father, but he doesn't respond.

Brendan returns and they help their father from the car, Mary holding their father's head down so he doesn't hit it on the top of the door. On the sidewalk, Mary takes her father's left arm and Brendan grabs his right and they start toward the brown house, arm in arm in arm. They seem like something out of the Wizard of Oz, Mary thinks, following the yellow brick road.

"Around the side," Brendan says as they come to the brown house.

Brendan leaves Mary and their father on the sidewalk and walks to the front door. He rings the bell once, then returns.

"There it is," he says, pointing to a small pile of leaves.

Slowly, they walk toward the pile. Mary is disappointed with Brendan. She'd expected a bigger pile for some reason, as if that would matter to her father, as if the number of leaves would make any difference. When they reach the pile, a window on the side of the house opens and a short haired woman with hoop earrings sticks her head out.

"Ready," she says. She's wearing a Boston College sweatshirt and her voice is high pitched.

"Let's do it," Brendan says.

The woman ducks back inside and a few seconds later *Cherry Pink and Apple Blossom White* begins to play. Mary has heard the song only once in her life, after she planned this outing and called Brendan to explain what she wanted to do and say that she couldn't do it without him. Reluctantly, he agreed. Since he stopped drinking, he almost always agreed, Mary had noticed

As the girl swings her bare leg out of the window, Mary removes the bottle of water from her pocket. She dumps the water onto the leaves and, indeed, a faint odor rises, not much, but maybe enough.

"Dad," Mary says. "Dad."

She drops two quarters, three dimes and a nickel in her father's pocket. She takes his hand, his hand that remembers, and places it into that same pocket. Brendan puts his hand over their father's pocket, trapping her father's hand, and then moving it so that the coins jingle.

"Look, Dad," she says. "Look."

Her father is distant and empty, and she needs him to focus, just this once, this one last time. Mary removes his coat thinking that the cold might shock him into some sort of awareness. Then she takes his head in her hands and points his nose at the leg dangling out the window. As she feels the weight of his head in her hands, she begins to feel foolish. She wonders again if this hasn't all been a big mistake. That maybe she did it merely to mitigate her own guilt, if it wasn't all for her after all. She wonders why she thought it would work in the first place.

Mary crunches some wet leaves with her foot and is about to call the whole thing off when she feels it, a tremor of sorts, then a tightening of muscles and, gradually, the lightening of the weight in her hands as her father, ever so slightly, lifts his head toward the girl's leg, still swinging playfully. Mary remains behind her father and can't see his eyes, and so will never know if they spark, but she feels his head rise and knows he must be aware of something. Something. She looks at Brendan, her wild and dutiful brother, and together they release their grip and back away from their father, who remains.

Tomorrow, she will surrender him to the nursing home, and they will both begin new lives – but that's tomorrow. Today there are trumpets playing and wet leaves on the ground and the bare leg of a pretty young girl in the window. Today it's almost Christmas, and her father's war is over, and there's a little bit of money in his pocket as he stands alone and for the last time on the broken precipice of possibility.

# THE PARTY

## Richard Kalich

"The Party" is a chapter from Richard Kalich's novel *Charlie P.* where we follow the comic misadventures of a singularly unique, comic and outlandish Everyman. At age three, when his father dies, he decides to overcome mortality by becoming immortal: by not living his life, he will live forever. Akin to other great American icons such as Sinclair Lewis's Babbit and Forrest Gump, Charlie P, while asocial and alienated, is, at the same time, at the heart of the American dream.

"Kalich represents the best in contemporary fiction. He has every chance to become – why not? – a living classical author."

—*Hooligan Magazine*, Moscow

Tired of being a stay-at-home and a couch potato, Charlie P gives a gala New Year's Eve party which not only he but nobody else attends. Even Charlie P was surprised at the turnout. To be sure, this is the best party he's never been to. The one he would least have wanted to miss.

The entire affair was catered by the world's greatest chefs, and platters of sumptuous foods were served by geishas in kimonos and men in black. Champagne flowed like April rain. Every guest was given a token of appreciation for not attending, diamonds and gold; and for those who didn't wear jewellery, thinking it ostentatious, or trade gold in the market, Picassos from the Blue period. And the entertainment was world class. From the Three Tenors, Nureyev and Fontaine, to rappers and hip-hop. From chart-breakers and the current pop, to has-beens and never-was's. Fireworks lit up the night sky before, during and after the party. Needless to say, there was something for everybody. For every taste and desire imaginable.

At long last Charlie P knew what it was to have the spotlight. To be the center of attention. If not for him this party that did not happen would never have taken place.

But what gave Charlie P the most satisfaction was the fact that all the people not attending the party got along charmed the pants, if not panties, off young career women in the bloom of youth. While hangers-on, freeloaders, and weak sons of strong fathers could be seen having serious and meaningful discussions with men of the cloth. And chronically cheating husbands and adulterous wives, who had fought tooth and nail over divorce settlements, alimony payments and child support for years, were now laughing together, making merry and dancing cheek to cheek. On a larger scale, and despite ancient enmities that had made for a thousand years of hatred, world rulers and Heads of State were making every effort to reconcile their differences; open lines of communication; enter into dialogue. And so, on this night, at Charlie P's party, at least, there was no such thing as separation of Church and State; East vs. West; men vs. women. Indeed, there was only commonality of purpose, good cheer, peace on earth and good will towards men.

For certain, at Charlie P's gala New Year's Eve party which didn't take place—happy times were here again. Still, by the night's end, Charlie P was visibly disappointed. The crowd had already filtered out, most rushing off to other parties, and other than a few tepid kisses on the cheek from the women, ceremonial hugs from the men, and the usual "see you next year"'s, Charlie P once again felt empty, alone, deserted. He certainly wasn't ready to relinquish the spotlight, stop being the host and center of attention. And, so, he began thinking about next year's party. No, it would not be a sequel of this year's event; a rehashing and recycling of the time-tested and familiar. Next year Charlie P decided that rather than be a small fish in a big pond, he would be a big fish in a small pond by giving his party in a soup kitchen for the hungry and homeless, the needy and disenfranchised. Not only so well. High rollers mixed with paupers, and aging playboys would he save a fortune by not having to wine and dine his guests with diamonds and gold, but all those unfortunates needed to be happy was a bowl of hot soup, a warm bed, a pair of sturdy thick-soled boots and a windbreaker for the ensuing winter months. Toss in a few extra dollars to keep them off the dole, and, rest assured, more than lukewarm kisses and perfunctory hugs, he would be adulated, venerated, possibly even canonized as a saint.

But what if all those people who didn't attend this year's party attend next year's party?

---

The story continues in *Central Park West Trilogy, Charlie P.* by Richard Kalich.

# BLUE AND UNASSUMING UNDER A CHRISTMAS STAR

## Jackie Mallon

### Author's note

Kat, a farmer's daughter from rural Ireland, and Edward, a preppy *Economist*-reading builder's son from Birmingham, met five years ago in London at an illustrious school for fashion design. Forced to collaborate on a project, they became unlikely friends and upon graduation, embarked upon an exploration of the "Bella Vita" in Milan, Italy. My debut novel, *Silk for the Feed Dogs*, follows the agreeable pair through the ruthless and hierarchical fashion system, as they design the course of their careers, talk Italian, and practice in the fine art of seduction, Italian-style.

In *Blue and Unassuming under a Christmas Star*, we find Kat a year later, landing in New York from Paris, where she and Edward have been living since leaving Milan. She is to meet Edward, who is arriving in town on the tail end of a work trip, at their hotel. Kat anticipates the kickoff of a glamorous holiday sojourn enjoying their friendship, the world-famous sights and revelling in the Big Apple's gung-ho conjuring of the Christmas spirit. But one mishap threatens to throw a damper on it...

—Jackie Mallon

She realizes she has left her phone on the AirTrain. A sign on the back of the cab driver's seat informs her the airport is fifteen miles from Midtown Manhattan. Therefore she is about seven and a half miles away from her phone, and light years away from Edward. He's stuck in Shanghai with no idea when he will board a flight. This she found out after landing at JFK. In a hurried voicemail message, he recounted a story about a lorry load of knit samples being stolen en route from the factory, leaving them with only thirty-five percent of the Spring collection. He would have to scramble to put everything into work again, and it was the night before he was supposed to leave, the night before he was supposed to join her for their glamorous Manhattan Christmas.

We couldn't organize a piss-up in a brewery, thinks Kat, looking out at the light snow flurrying between one lane of traffic and the next.

From the hotel she will call him. What if it's night-time there? She'll write him an email briefly explaining the loss of her phone and describe a hastily composed itinerary for the day. Then she'll make her way back to the hotel and call him again around lunchtime. Otherwise she'll just see him whenever he checks in. Whatever day he arrives. She looks down at her lap. She has been picking the skin on her thumb which she does when she is anxious. The distant Manhattan skyline stretches out alongside the cab like a misty hedgerow.

"Do you know the cross street, Miss?"

"Um, no, just the address, 204 West 29th?" The driver doesn't look too impressed with her organizational skills either.

Why isn't the street address enough here? And why isn't the price advertised the price you end up paying? She is already fretting about what tip to give him.

The hotel lobby is medieval dark, dotted with untreated wood and hunks of dulled metal slabs edged with rivets posing as furniture. The soft lighting is mostly provided by the rows of laptops on low tables. She waits for a well-shaven man in a narrow cut suit to finish with another guest. He approaches beaming a wide, white-toothed welcome.

"Hello. My name's Kat Connelly. I'm checking in."

He studies the computer screen. "I don't seem to have anything by that name."

"Oh, of course not! It'll be under Edward Brandreth. He made the reservation. Two single rooms."

Wide, white-toothed understanding. He hits several keys. "No, I'm sorry, we have nothing under that name either. Are you sure you're in the right hotel?"

The piece of paper in her right hand shows the name and address of this hotel, her handwriting. "It is—I mean, it should be. It was booked weeks ago. Are you sure? Can you just check again?"

No white teeth this time. "Do you have a confirmation or booking number?"

She hadn't thought to print it out. "My friend Edward booked."

He taps repeatedly the same key. "Wait up. I have a Brandreth for tomorrow night. Two single rooms. Ten days."

"Oh, thank God! You had me there! I knew he couldn't be that dizzy—I mean, dizzy enough, obviously, as the booking should include tonight, but at least all's not lost. Phew!" With no effort she matches the width of his smile. "That's a relief. Can I have a room for tonight, please?"

His smile goes again and the lobby darkens. She watches him shake his head. "I'm sorry, miss, it's the week before Christmas, we're full up."

"I'll take a double, whatever you've got. I don't mind paying more."

His demeanour softens and he leans in, his elbows on the counter. "Girl, you're going to have trouble getting in anywhere no matter how much money you got." His accent had eased down-home. "I mean, maybe a Holiday Inn in the boroughs but, seriously, come on, a room tonight? New York is busier than a one-legged dog with fleas."

There it is: the calamity she feels has been looming since leaving the airport. Alone in New York City with nowhere to sleep. She and Edward should have figured out alternative arrangements in case something went wrong, because with their track record something always goes wrong. It seems inconceivable she didn't get a copy of the confirmation email. Instead of discussing the details of the booking, they had spent most of their last phone conversation giddily quoting Christmas movies:

"If it's Serendipity, I'll get in two hours after you. I'll meet you just left of Miracle on 34th Street."

"Can you believe it, Jack Skellington? Next stop, shopping in Christmastown!"

"'What is it you want, Mary? What do you want? You want the moon? Just say the word and I'll throw a lasso around it and pull it down. Hey. That's a pretty good idea. I'll give you the moon, Mary.'"

"'I'll take it. Then what?'"

"'Well, then you can swallow it, and it'll all dissolve, see... and the moonbeams would shoot out of your fingers and your toes and the ends of your hair!'"

Weighing the pointlessness of sitting in a hotel where she is not a guest versus the aimlessness of wandering the city alone, Kat chooses the latter. She'll be able to think as she walks; neurons will wake up, band together, and storm her cranium to arrive a solution. She curses the people of Shanghai as a bunch of Scrooges trying to spoil their holiday merriment, all over a few sweaters.

*If I could work my will, every idiot who goes about with 'Merry Christmas' on his lips, should be boiled with his own pudding, and buried with a stake of holly through his heart!*

The desk clerk agrees to hold her luggage until the evening. "It's against hotel policy if you're not a guest but, geez, far be it from me to contribute to your troubles, child. Quick, leave it there, I'll pretend I don't see." Theatrically he turns away. "I see nothing!"

Taking a deep breath, she steps out into the circular currents of snow and asks someone directions for Fifth Avenue. Considering herself well-travelled, she is surprised how much New York intimidates her with its size and noise and brashness. What becomes immediately clear is she's not wearing the right shoes. Her toes are clenching in retreat from the damp that's seeping through the seams of her vintage leather. She studies the feet that pass; even the lower legs of the women wearing dainty pencil skirts culminate in one of two ways: a quilted nylon blob, somewhere in the vicinity of a ski boot gathered by drawstring at the calf, or a garishly patterned rubber boot resembling children's footwear that waggles about the leg. Both serve to annihilate the line of calf to ankle. Parisians would opt for being born with a cloven hoof rather than have that happen, regardless of the weather, she thinks, then reminds herself that this is the land where chic lags behind comfort. In every company she has ever worked, jersey knit, the ultimate leisure fabric, sold best in the US market. In her line of business, she can't help but compare how people dress from place to place and what they tote, forming opinions, reaching conclusions.

She catches a glimpse of herself in a window. Hands clasped before her, she looks like she's praying. She resolves to be less of a blip moving erratically across a grid and more attuned to her surroundings.

She wonders how she ever found her way about or did anything before smartphones, and then gives a grunt. Smartphones render their owners idiots.

Even as her thinking desperately turns to public pay phones, she notices how many people are bearing down on her at speed, heads bent over their own personal screens and keypads. Pate first, they charge; a herd of headlong bovines branded with Apple or Samsung. A telephone booth, there has to be one or two left. The words *telephone booth* sound so cozy as she trudges on, the prospect of curling up in intimate seclusion for a chat with a friend so appealing. It suddenly sounds as archaic a term as *hat box, penny farthing,* and *powder puff.* Still, there just has to be one or two left.

A massive stone building, beautiful, opens up on her left with sculptures of robed men lining the ledges against the sky, four sets of twin columns flanking tall arched entrances, and two stone lions on podiums. The brave pair wear wreathes around their necks and matching jaunty red satin bows tied at the throat. Carved into the stone in large capitals are the words New York Public Library. A library is for the people, she reasons, a bricks and mortar font of information left over from the pre-Information Age, immobile, uninvolved with satellite signals, and from what she can see, open. Hurrah for the old world! She climbs the steps, past the lions surely guarding the last of the city's public telephones, heartened by the sight of the gold and red Christmas tree twinkling warmly just inside the central archway. A security guard steps forward, asks to search her bag. He peeks inside and taps the leather reassuringly to move her on.

"Can you tell me where the public telephones are, please?"

"Payphones, you mean?" He smiles. "Huh, now, there's a question. Do we still have them even?" He looks around, purses his lips. Without warning he calls out, his voice echoing through archways, up stairways and crashing off ceilings "Hey... Hey Curtis! Yo, we got any payphones up in here?"

When those echoes subside, new ones ripple in from a hidden Curtis. "Yeah, bro. Saw them the other day. By the children's section."

The security guard points over his shoulder to the right. "Just through there, the second room."

Her eyes glisten with unspoken thanks as Curtis's voice soars in again. "They all broken though. Somebody needs to make it their business to call a repair guy."

The sight of her downcast face touches the security guard, compels him to offer what he thinks is a serviceable solution. "Miss, we have Wi-Fi though. On every floor, in every reading room and even in the grounds outside." With a nod and smile, his duty done, he beckons the next visitor forward. Kat heads back down the steps to be reclaimed by the Fifth Avenue throng.

The ground is laced with white now. As she walks she imagines herself at the centre of a Christmas movie scene, the city's noises, already dulled by snowfall, overtaken by some soaring Henry Mancini soundtrack with added jingle bells, the cameras panning out to focus on her lone black figure growing smaller on the city's grand grid, progressing uptown, yes, uptown because now she is at 49th Street. She finds the architecture miniaturizing, yet when she manages to forget for a second her predicament, it's uplifting too. She could be protagonist or extra in any story here, feel like a star or be extra anonymous. On impulse she reaches out and touches the expensive plaid sleeve of a passing woman's coat.

"I'm terribly sorry, would I be able to use your cell phone briefly to make a call? I'm alone in the city and—" The woman flicks Kat's fingers from the plaid without stopping. Kat tries this with three more strangers. An older woman steps back alarmed which makes Kat fade embarrassed into the crowd, her heart pounding. A teenager tells her to get lost. Finally a man pauses and listens to her tale with his head cocked to one side. At first it might be a business pitch he's hearing but presently Kat detects in his eyes a glimmer of compassion. Then at the mention of Shanghai, he splutters "Yeah, right!" and bolts with a flap of his topcoat. Bolstered, however, Kat fishes ten dollars from her purse and holds it in both hands as she approaches another man in a suit, tie and topcoat. These corporate types seem to be the most amenable to her intrusion, and she ignores her uneasiness when she thinks how it must look: young female approaching older businessman leading to a sidewalk exchange of money.

"Listen, I'll help you out, but if my wife calls, I need to answer it, you got that? She's been chasing me all day and I've sent her to voicemail four times." He looks down the street, both ways, turns his lapel up. "She is *not* happy." He waves away her money and hands her earbuds. "Use these. I'll keep hold of the phone." Glancing up gratefully and with clumsy fingers, she inserts them in her ears, pulls the same piece of paper that contains the hotel address from her pocket and punches in Edward's cell phone number. Her forefinger picks a shard of skin from around her thumbnail and she barely registers the sting of it as she listens to the dial tone. *Curse him to Almighty for not answering.* She can picture him squinting at the screen, lifting it up to study the number, pursing his contrary little lips, then replacing it on a desk with a sniff and turning back to what he was doing. It goes to voicemail and she feels like hurling the stranger's phone into the traffic.

"Hey, it's Edward. Why are you disturbing me with a phone call? Nowadays it's much less invasive to text. Oh, while you're here, go on then, leave a message. If you must."

BEEP. Barely managing to keep from shrieking, she launches breathlessly into her message, "Bloody hell, Edward! You booked the hotel for tomorrow night, not tonight. I'm stranded in New York with no place to sleep! I've lost my phone and—" There is a noise, not a promising one. The phone gulps and she realizes the man has shot off in the other direction with the phone to his ear, the chord of his earbuds dangling between her fingers. "Hey! Wait, please! I was in the middle of talking! WAIT please, I'm begging you!" She runs after him and pulls at his coat, his sleeve, his flapping scarf; he jerks away. "No it's no one, honey. I promise. Don't be silly, it's just some crazy person on Fifth Avenue. Tis the season, after all. Look, I'll be home early; we'll go to our place." He turns, mouths *sorry* and hurries off.

She drops onto the steps of St Patrick's Cathedral. Mentally exhausted and with nowhere to sleep, she now recognizes the lumbering juggernaut of jetlag encroaching from the peripheries. The dusting of snow on the step turns to water under her rear, no doubt marking her best coat in an unfortunate, truly homeless-looking way. Over her shoulder a long queue snakes from the door of the neo-Gothic cathedral around the block, a mixture of prayer book and guidebook believers anticipating the exalted stained glass, the Tiffany-designed altar, the lofty marble columns fanning out like palm leaves to the ceiling, and the *pietà* that's three times the size of Michelangelo's *Pietà*. She thinks about joining them and curling up just inside under the holy water fountain till morning. She could light a candle and leave it to the heavens to seal her fate. If Edward were here he would say, "You don't come to New York to go to church, Kat, you can do that anytime. I personally don't do religion unless I have drink in me. See? I'm more Irish than you think."

She picks herself up and crosses the street alongside a trio of singing Santas bearing a Salvation Army donation bucket. Their accelerated harmonies of "O Little Town of Bethlehem" make shoppers dance and sway.

She fights to extract herself from behind a group of Italians who have halted smack dab in the middle of the pavement. They are all dressed in the same quilted jacket but in different colours and resemble a little barricade of activated airbags. She attempts unsuccessfully to go around them and the old irritation arises in her even though it has been over a year since she left. Loitering with lack of intent she called it. You can take the Italian out of the piazza but you can't take the piazza out of the Italian.

"*Permesso?*" She sighs dramatically. "*Mi fate passare?*"

Looks of surprise. The airbags are deactivated. "*Prego, Signorina!*" Just like that, she has removed the look of the tourist from each of their faces by generously placing them on familiar territory. Sure enough, she feels their eyes work their way down the length of her and make the return journey.

"*Mille grazie,*" she says haughtily, passing through their centre. A few steps later, she, like them, stops short, infuriating those behind her.

Of course, there is its stature, but she is already used to the bigness of big here. That isn't what makes it special. It is the inch-by-inch attention to detail on such a scale. The Rockefeller Christmas tree. There isn't a pine needle that doesn't sparkle against the fuchsia-lit facade of the skyscraper behind it. It is the Taylor-Burton diamond of Christmas trees. It symbolizes ambition, hope, confidence.

Kat has to believe this energizing trio must surge through the city all year round but at Christmas they really come into their own, accompanied by French horns, gussied up with flashing lights and tied with bows. Quiet confidence is an oxymoron here, quiet hope akin to hopelessness, quiet ambition no ambition at all. That must be the New York way from what she has observed. Just four hours since landing and she marvels at the unapologetic volume of people's voices. Everyone's an announcer. Italians yell at each other in the street, a barrage of obscenities or the same predictable *Ciao Bellissima,* but New Yorkers make you privy to the full-throated details of divorce settlements, bank accounts, therapy sessions, troubled childhoods, this verbal release ushering them on to greater things. All the neuroses of a Woody Allen film seem to sputter from the city's orifices like natural waste, better out than in. Beside her, with the Rockefeller spectacle as his backdrop, a man on his cell phone describes being audited by the tax authorities, having his screenplay rejected by a famous director and getting hit by a yellow cab—and no health insurance!—all in the same week. Then he turns and offers her a toothpaste commercial grin. Built on the smoldering remains of trauma and dysfunction rises the city of eternal hope; white teeth in the face of adversity.

She decides she would do well to learn a thing or two from them and quit being such a defeatist. All she needs is a room for the night. There are infinite possibilities that could yet unfold. A brass band bursts buoyantly into "Good King Wenceslas" and she feels grateful she didn't leave her wallet behind instead of the phone. She drinks in one last view of the tree and adjusts her thinking. I am in control of my own destiny. Look around! Here I am in the heart of Manhattan despite less than ideal circumstances but how can I complain if I am at the centre of the world? This isn't called the Empire State for nothing.

The corner of Fifty-Fourth and Fifth offers prime people-watching opportunities. New Yorkers have a possessiveness to their stride; every purpose-filled step is a flag planted in the patch of cement they have landed on. Even though their foot abandons it immediately in search of pastures new, for that fleeting moment, that square meter of the city is all theirs, a successful mini takeover bid. Kat tries to mimic this and with renewed resolve, enters two nearby hotels and requests a room. Both times the hotel staff wear the same looks of worried confusion that the previous hotel clerk wore.

Then Kat sees it, blue and unassuming under a Christmas star of neon fixed to a lamp post: a public telephone. It's clear it's working because a man is talking into it, and quite animatedly at that. The brass band plays on and Kat blesses their merry souls. She almost tingles with the certainty that this time she will get through, that Edward will have listened to her truncated message and will be on alert for her to call again. Dare she hope it?

As she draws near, there is a new noise discernible above all the rest, a sound like the animalistic grunt boxers make when they suffer repeated blows to the head. The telephone user's voice. "Look behind me, he says. Behind me, motherfucker? I ain't no fool. Put your head back in your Facebook. Tell me, does this train run express? Huh, does it? Holy shit, this carriage stinks." His head, wrapped in a purple bandanna that's tucked under an orange baseball cap embellished with badges, jerks back with the delivery of every short sentence as if with the force of a punch. He pokes the air for emphasis. "It's the Uptown train I need, motherfucker. Get out my way!"

He removes the phone from his ear and stares the mouthpiece down. With his lips pulled into two taut slivers, he mutters between clenched teeth and strikes the corner of the payphone with the receiver, a gut-wrenching noise, simultaneously slamming his fist against the numbers, once, twice, three times. Kat is beside him. "No-no, please, no don't do that, no..." She seizes the receiver, prizing his fingers off it one by one. His hand falls limp. Puzzlement knits his features. He frees the telephone receiver and runs off, turning to look back at her as he cuts through the crowd.

Close to tears, Kat hangs up the receiver. She can feel the pulse at her wrist stampeding. She lifts the phone again, her body slack with pessimism, and holds it to her ear. Not a sound. Probably wasn't even working in the first place.

The bobbing and curtsying sound of the brass band can be heard from several blocks away, mocking her.

*And the Grinch said, "Blast this Christmas music... it's joyful AND triumphant."*

Up ahead, a sign propped against a homeless man's knees catches her eye, and its gallows humour manages to draw from her the vaguest smile: "I always wanted to be someone but I see now I should have been more specific."

"I love your sign," she tells him, yearning for conversation. "Profound."

"Could you spare some change please, Miss?"

She can't resist asking his name. Sean. Sean Donnelly. He is a down-on-his-luck corn-fed All-American boy with an all-round good Irish name. His sign informs her he needs bus fare back to Kansas. She empties her purse.

Sean counts the different sized coins she has poured into his hand and looks up at her. "Sixty-four cents? You're giving me sixty-four cents?"

"Is that all that's there?" Back in her purse, nothing; she fishes in her pockets, nothing. "I'm sorry, that's all I have. I haven't been to an ATM machine yet."

"Man, I cannot believe it. What the fuck am I supposed to do with that?"

In Sean Kat recognizes not a point of conversation anymore but the repository for all her frustrations. "Give that money back, you little shit. Go on, hand it over." She holds out her hand and several shoppers gasp. "Come on, it's Christmas, let it go," says one, "you won't miss it." "You mind your own business," she hisses, bracing herself menacingly at the passers-by who walk on, shaking their heads and muttering, "Some people have no sense of charity, and at this time of year…" When Kat turns back to Sean, he wears a look somewhere between amusement and challenge.

"Well, now."

"You're disrespecting me. You don't deserve my money. I didn't have to give you anything, I could have walked on by like everyone else. This is not a place for pennies, I can see that. Well, fair enough, give it back, come on. Hold out for some of those great big dollar bills you're waiting for. And good luck to you!" She looks at the yoghurt pot he uses to collect money, gives it a light kick. It contains silver and copper but only two notes. "It looks like they're harder to come by than you think."

"You're a feisty wee one, aren't ye?" His accent evokes less of the Kansas cornfields and more of the Wicklow Mountains. "If you want your money back you'll have to come in here and take it." He puts the hand holding the coins down deep into his sleeping bag.

"You're not even American. You and your transatlantic false accent."

"Who broke your train set? Don't you have no Christmas spirit? You're in the wrongest place on earth then, aren't you?"

"Bah humbug."

She hunkers down and, leaning against the wall of a men's luxury tie store, she breathes in deep, falls silent. She secretly enjoyed that outburst, probably because Sean is the first company she's had since she left Charles de Gaulle. She eases up and finds him to be a decent listener as she confides in him her run of poor luck.

"There's a YMCA on Forty-Seventh that might have vacancies if you don't mind the bedbugs, cockroaches and constant smell of marijuana, as well as the long walk down *The Shining* corridor to get to the shared bathroom. It's where I go when I'm feeling flush after a win on the horses, it being a smidgen closer than the Waldorf Astoria." He smiles wryly and produces from his sleeping bag the latest iPhone which with a swipe of his finger casts a festive glow onto his features. He hands it over. "Call them."

"You got the newest one. How? There's even a waiting list."

"I took my sleeping bag and camped outside the Apple store overnight. I got the second last one."

The Hispanic lady who answers the phone tells Kat there are no vacancies but sometimes there are no-shows and she should stop by that evening around seven when they give out unused beds on a first come, first serve basis. It's the most encouraging news she's had since she landed. She visits an ATM machine and drops twenty dollars into Sean's yoghurt pot. Then adds another ten in exchange for making a second call to Edward.

This time she expects no response and isn't disappointed. She leaves a message stating that she will be at the YMCA Vanderbilt at seven and will hopefully stay there that night. "Otherwise I'll be temporarily residing in a cardboard box on Fifth Avenue—cross street?—Fifty-Sixth beside a nice Irishman called Sean whose phone I'm using to make this call that you can't be bothered to answer. But the cardboard box will be Bergdorf Goodman's largest because this was supposed to be a glamorous holiday after all, and it will have oodles of tinsel draped over it because, God forbid, I lose the Christmas spirit. Hope you're warm and cosy toasty with a dirty martini at arm's length. Ciao."

"Ah, sarcasm. I do miss me ma."

While Sean slides his iPhone into the depths of his sleeping bag, Kat rises and hops about to warm up. "I can only imagine what else you've got down there."

He flashes a crooked smile. "It's not the most subtle of advances I've heard but what the hell, cease imagining immediately, woman, and hop on in." He lowers the zipper and holds open the mouth of the sleeping bag. "I'll show you mine if—"

"Oh, God, I didn't mean that! I mean, I wasn't, God, total embarrassment."

"Ach, I'm only messin' with ye."

She smiles. "Right. Well, I'm going to have to keep moving or I'll catch pneumonia. Although of sturdy stock, today I'm being sorely tested. Care for a walk?"

"Can't, doll. Guy's gotta make a living." Sean's American accent is back. He spirits the bills from the yoghurt pot, shakes the coins up and looks expectantly into the faces that pass. She wishes him merry Christmas and melds with the crowd.

Soon she is in the thick of Manhattan's fanciest shops, passing Prada, Henri Bendel, Gucci, Tiffany, Dolce & Gabbana. Street carts sell roasted chestnuts and hotdogs but she can't account for the smell of cinnamon everywhere. It hangs under her running nose. Eartha Kitt purrs from every doorway, "Santa cutie, fill my stocking with a duplex and checks. Sign your X on the line..." She should feel right at home; it's the New York equivalent of strolling along Via Montenapoleone or rue du Faubourg Saint-Honoré as she and Edward had done so often in the past. She wishes he was beside her, the sight of luxury goods making her feel surprisingly melancholy. The window displays are like spreads from her favourite fashion magazines, opulent optical feasts curated with an eye for theatre, and yet, she can reduce them to towers of expensive white-frosted clutter in a second.

She joins the little assembly of fashion devotees paying homage outside the first window of Bergdorf Goodman. The window is as large as a room, with all the pomp and ceremony of a Broadway stage. Kat's eyes gorge on human-sized marionettes brandishing trumpets, frilled candy-striped lampshades resembling the petticoat skirts of Toulouse-Lautrec's dancers, crystal-flecked Venetian masks and studded pink suede shoes, little caped drummer girls, bunches of swollen grapes tumbling from goblets and confetti-flecked doughnuts as big as wreathes suspended above vintage cars; velvet purses under icicles and whipped cream pies arranged in a still-life with jellyfish, tapestries and reptiles; Audrey Hepburn's pearls are strewn across the leather and chrome of a Harley Davison parked in a glacially lit grotto next to a stuffed peacock; giant slices of cake with chocolate dipped strawberries may have been made of papier-mâché, but Kat would eat them all anyway. This glorious lack of cohesion makes her want to lick every window. She craves all of it, her nose to the glass in the hope of at least smelling it. She hadn't known this ravenous consumer was rushing about inside her, clamouring to get out.

A liveried horseman in a frosted, duck-egg blue carriage pulled by a horse sprouting feathers from his forehead and a lei around his neck passes close to the sidewalk. Kat turns around just as the lascivious clap of manure hitting Manhattan's tarmac rings out. A voice at her shoulder says, "Kat, how is it possible that livestock still know just where to find you, all these years after leaving the farm?"

"Edward!" The heads of the Bergdorf Goodman pilgrims swivel in unison. She squeezes him so tightly he yelps.

"You're throttling me, you daft apeth! It hasn't been that long. I just saw you a couple of weeks ago!"

"Are you joking? Did you get my messages? I've been worrying all day. How did you know where to find me?"

He winks. "As Cary Grant says to Deborah Kerr, "'If you can paint, I can walk—'" She joins in, "'—anything can happen!' An Affair to Remember!" She squeezes his arm. "Yep, you're real."

"As real as Christmas, and twice as camp."

"But still, how did you know in all of New York I'd be here?"

"It required no great calculation. I know you too well. I knew you'd stare moony-eyed for hours at these windows. Of course I did. What else would you do on your first day, the zoo? I'm not saying you're predictable or anything. So I sat in the Plaza Hotel by the window and waited with a piping hot toddy for my trouble. I was getting worried. Would I be able to see you when it got dark? Lo and behold, I stepped outside to smoke a ciggie and saw you turn the corner right at the window that has the perfume bottles sliding down the mini ski slope. What a relief. I've picked up the cargo, crisis averted, now, let's go. I've wangled a night at the Plaza for us from a rather charming gentleman I met. You'll meet him too. Incidentally, do you know how much those suites cost? Cripes, try our whole holiday budget and then some! See, turns out I made a little mistakeroo with our hotel booking but don't worry about it. They serve the best sidecars in the upstairs bar here and we can dine on truffle-flavoured popcorn—what are you looking at me like that for?"

"But I was planning on staying with the cockroaches at the YMCA, dining on the lingering smell of marijuana?"

"Suit yourself but it's really rather nice over here. Aren't you cold? You look a wreck. Why is the arse of your coat all black? You look like you've slept on a park bench. This is the Plaza we're talking about!"

"Did you see the Valentino shoes in that third window?"

The bar upstairs at the Plaza is doused in crimson light. Everything dances and flickers, down below the magnificent chandeliers sparkle in the art deco foyer, its domed ceiling of sepia stained glass florals trellised with black shedding a benign serenity over the heads below. The Christmas tree is trimmed with ropes of crystals and shimmering glass balls and at the heart of all these lights, beams, sparkles and glimmers, Kat and Edward's eyes dance as their conversation meanders.

Outside, the white-gloved doormen welcome guests from town cars. The horse drawn carriages have bottlenecked at the entrance to Central Park. Yellow cabs circle the Pulitzer fountain arriving and departing the hotel's red carpeted front steps in steady numbers. At the centre of it, Pomona, the goddess of abundance, with her basket of fruit raised, looks off contentedly, to the right of Kat and Edward, beyond the trees into Central Park, past the ice rink and the Jacqueline Kennedy-Onassis reservoir and to the dark empty grassless greens of Strawberry Fields and Sheep Meadow, now completely white.

———————————

More about Kat and Edward in *Silk for the Feed Dogs* by Jackie Mallon.

# NO TRUCE FOR CHRISTMAS

## Donald Finnaeus Mayo

### Author's note

First known in the West for its spices, the island of Timor lies in
South East Asia between Indonesia and Australia. For much of its
recent history it has been ignored by the world at large, its political
and administrative geography a consequence of the crude manner
in which European colonial powers carved up the region in their
pursuit of commodities.

That all changed in December 1975, following a series of
political upheavals from Mozambique to Vietnam via Lisbon that
caused the Indonesian government to view its sleepy neighbour in
a fresh, menacing light. For East Timorese people such as seventeen
year old Francesca, it was going to be a Christmas they would never
forget...

—Donald Finnaeus Mayo

---

F rancesca walked down the dusty street, between the pot-
holed track and what was left of the crumbling pavement. Her feet kept jarring when she forgot to compensate
for the four inch height difference between the two surfaces,

which periodically evaporated in the remains of the puddles that had washed parts of the path away.

She yanked her satchel up onto her shoulder, almost ripping the seam under her armpit as she did. The satchel strap caught itself between the two enamel badges pinned to her left breast – the one the St Xavier's school badge, the other her prefect's pin, bestowed upon her just a few weeks ago.

Her mother had already warned her she wasn't going to replace the three simple white button-up cotton shirts until the new term; Francesca would have to make them last until Christmas. Likewise with the dark blue skirts, although here Francesca suspected the virtue of modesty might overcome that of thrift. Fortunately, she'd had new sandals only a month ago and they'd taken the precaution of allowing plenty of room for growth. Actually, it was more comfortable to remain on the road altogether.

She thought about how much easier it was to learn English if you'd grasped Portuguese first, about the table tennis championships and the badminton tournament in which she was currently a promising quarter finalist with a very good chance of going all the way, and, of course, about rehearsals for the Christmas Carol service which had the added attraction of involving boys from neighbouring St Michael's.

Then she allowed her thoughts to wander to Miguel; his long, sensuous fingers delicately wrapped around a pen as he wrestled with a mathematical problem. Her friends dismissed him as a dullard, it was only Francesca, it seemed, who could see through the spectacles taped up at one join and sitting wonkily across his slightly prominent nose, into the wonderful mind. Miguel was a serious person, and this, she suspected, was what made her friends so contemptuous of him and caused him to be the object of so much teasing. He had the air of making people feel shallow in his company, and naturally they didn't like it.

With Francesca the effect was exactly the opposite; the more he spoke, the more she yearned to learn about the world beyond the narrow confines of Dili. Of late, he had begun to show an interest in politics, and although he was careful not to express his sympathies in public, he had confided in her how he was a firm supporter of the emerging Fretilin administration, and had even considered leaving the increasingly chaotic Dili to join a Falintil fighting patrol in the hills. The knowledge both thrilled and terrified her, for awkward, clumsy Miguel seemed such an unlikely soldier. He was so wise yet still so vulnerable, and had thought life through so clearly whilst being only marginally less sheltered than her. It was hard, straddling the comfortable certainties of St. Xavier's, all masses, badminton competitions and English lessons, with the grown-up anxiety concerning her country's precarious future. Did Miguel really know what he was letting himself into getting involved with Falintil? Should she even be talking to him?

Her home lay another block and a half away; a stilted house set in the middle of an unplanned sprawl at the edge of town. It was half kampong, half townhouse, a fringe community that bore the aura of a people yet to be fully convinced of the benefits of emerging from the bush. A single power line offered intermittent supplies of electricity to run a small refrigerator, an ancient TV (not that there was ever anything to watch), and a single low wattage light bulb suspended from a stick her father had wedged between two beams holding up the ceiling.

Francesca's mother was waiting for her, squatting as ever over an open fire cooking a cauldron of rice into which she'd stirred a few root vegetables and some spices. It had been over a week since they'd had any meat; they were all uncomfortably aware it was soon time to decide whether to sacrifice another egg laying chicken to the pot on top of the one that had already been earmarked for Christmas Day. The final call would be with her mother; when she gave the word Antonio or Marco would be summoned to wring the specified bird's neck, pluck its feathers and present the carcass for the first of the four meals to which her mother insisted a chicken had to run.

Antonio was already home, stretched out on the hammock, no doubt exhausted from the rigors of filling yet another drawn out day in the futile pursuit of work. Eight months of idleness had left him cynical and disillusioned, and Francesca instinctively shuffled her bag across her shoulder so that the evidence of her industry wouldn't attract his wounded scorn. Antonio had an answer for everything and a solution for nothing, so that while he blamed everyone for the state they found themselves in: the useless Portuguese, the bellicose Indonesians harassing their borders, the well-meaning but ineffectual Fretilin trying to make some semblance of a government out of a rag-tag resistance movement, he couldn't rouse himself to do anything, because everything was pointless anyway and run by a bunch of corrupt incompetents who had no idea what it was really like to be eighteen and stuck in a no-hope dump like Dili.

Francesca knew her mother worried about Antonio, and particularly the influence he was exerting on Marco, at fourteen still deeply impressed by the apparent worldliness of his elder brother. She could hear Marco out at the back, the tap-tap-tap of the football against his foot as he honed his ball skills between the two trees at either end of their small dusty yard. She didn't bother going round to greet him, but marched straight across the porch, acknowledging Antonio's supercilious stare with a brief nod, to open the spring shutter with the green gauze netting stretched across its frame against mosquitoes. She guessed she had about forty minutes for her homework until her mother summoned her to help with the chores; twenty minutes for her English composition, fifteen minutes on the advent passage they were studying from St. Luke's gospel and a quick five minutes, if she was lucky, to take a look at tomorrow's algebra.

In the end, she was left undisturbed a full hour and a quarter until her father arrived back from work. As soon as she heard him chain his bicycle to the corner post holding up the house she put her books away and went in search of his slippers and the cup of sweet tea her mother would have waiting for him. Francesca listened as he ascended the steps, pausing momentarily to berate Antonio for his idleness, to enter the room holding his battered shoulder bag. His face seemed as weary as the worn-out leather, his eyes emanating a deep tiredness as he reached over to kiss her once on each cheek.

"And how is my little scholar today?" he asked as she presented him with his slippers and tea.

"Oh, I'm fine, thank you Daddy. How was your work?"

"Pretty dreadful," her father replied grimly, settling himself into the single threadbare armchair and taking a sip from the proffered cup of tea. There was a quality to their relationship that had enabled her father, from the time Francesca had been a tiny girl, to expound freely upon whatever was on his mind. It was a habit he engaged in with none of her siblings, and it had become customary for him to unburden himself to her, perhaps as a more convenient and somewhat less trouble-some alternative to the confessional box.

"It's not so much the situation at the station," her father continued, "as the situation all around us." Here her father waved his one free hand to signify their entire visible world. "There are reports of all sorts of trouble around the border, the Fretilin boys are getting really antsy. They've been bombarding us all day with updates, and at lunchtime a whole delegation of them came in and commandeered the studio. Three of them sat down in the newsroom and started bashing out speeches which they ordered the presenters to read out on air between Christmas Carols. Inflammatory stuff, too."

"Did you broadcast it?"

"Of course we did. We had no choice. But I tell you one thing, I don't want to be around that place if the Indonesians do decide to invade. It'll be the first thing they go for."

"Is it safe?" asked Francesca, suddenly concerned for the vulnerable figure in front of her.

Her father shrugged his shoulders and took another sip from his tea. Beneath the bitter cheer, she could see the lines of worry chiselling away at the edges of his eyes and mouth. "What's safe these days?" he replied. "I certainly wouldn't want to be in those newsreaders' shoes after today, but no one knows my name. Sometimes it's not such a bad thing to go about your business quietly behind the scenes. In times like these, drawing attention to yourself can be asking for a whole load of trouble."

"Do you think they will invade?"

Her father shook his head dismissively, as if he had been asked this question many times, considered the likelihood from all angles, and ruled out the prospect. "No, I don't think so. They'll continue harassing us along the border, and I don't doubt they'll try to rig the elections if we ever get round to having them, but I don't think they'll come in en masse. They'll undermine us from within to get what they want, that's more their style."

"Antonio says they've got the forces lined up to march straight in."

"Antonio should be careful of shooting his mouth off when he doesn't know what he's talking about." Her father's voice was sharp, the anger overlaying a concern for whom, Francesca wondered. Antonio? Himself? The family? "Besides," her father continued, his voice softening, "it's one thing to invade a country, quite another to hold it. Those Falintil troops are dug in pretty deep and they're well-armed. They could give the Indonesians a real run for their money, especially in the hills."

"It might not stop them trying," pointed out Francesca.

"True," conceded her father, "but the Indonesians are realists. The last thing they want to get sucked into is another Vietnam. Those hills would soak up an awful lot of troops. I'm not saying they couldn't do it, or they won't do it eventually, but my bet is they won't go down the hard way until they've tried the easier routes and failed. Anyway, I've had a bellyful of politics for one day. What's your mother cooking for supper?"

"Vegetables and some rice, I think," replied Francesca, averting her eyes in shame at such a paltry offering.

"Hopefully it won't be boiled yams again."

"I don't think so."

"Thank God for that, I think I'm going to turn into one if I eat any more. Go on, you'd better run along and give her a hand. Don't worry about me, I can look after myself."

Reluctantly, Francesca did as she was bid, stopping only at the doorway where she turned to glance over at him once more before relinquishing her time as intellectual equal to don the drab mantle of unpaid house servant. She saw him shut his eyes and rub the lids in exhaustion, as if he could massage away not only his own tiredness but the clouds gathering over all their heads.

 She was curled up on her mattress against the wall nearest the stove when the first shells exploded at two o'clock in the morning, dramatically proving her father's optimistic predictions wrong. Although the first salvo landed over a mile away, it was the loudest and most forceful sound she had ever heard. The shock wave seemed to split the planks from the beams, causing the four-inch nails holding the frame of the house in place to rattle like so many rotten pegs in an old peasant woman's mouth. At the same time, its brittle force pierced the warm bubble of her dream, a sequence unbound by the constraints of linear logic or cause and effect, in which she and Miguel walked along the beach and played half-naked in the river. There was a sensuous quality to the dream that had she been true in her devoutness would have left her feeling ashamed and impure. As it was, her first thought was to resent this rude interruption for wrenching her away from such a delicious paradise, a thought quickly followed by the knowledge that the world had come to an end.

 The first explosion was followed by five more, followed by a pause long enough for her to wonder whether she had imagined the whole thing and it was a continuation of her dream with Miguel, the divine conclusion punishing her for her sins of the flesh. Then another salvo came, this time closer. By now the entire household was up, shouting above the squawk of chickens and the barking from chained dogs. Her father stumbled into the room, his pyjamas silhouetted in the doorway seeming only to heighten his aura of vulnerability. At that moment she knew, before she even caught his dazed expression, that he would not be able to protect them as up until now he always had; that this phenomenal terror closing in on them was something his fragile body was powerless to resist.

Each explosion sent shockwaves that reverberated through her, jarring vital organs of whose existence she was only now becoming fully conscious, so that on top of the deafening noise that made any kind of thought or intellectual response completely impossible, there was a sense of physical violation that assaulted, overwhelmed and shattered her most private being. It wasn't possible to stand up to this barrage; all you could do was seek out the nearest corner or hole and cover your head with your arms. So this was what people meant when they talked about being reduced to quivering jelly.

"They're coming, aren't they?" she said to her father once the noise from the latest explosion had abated.

"Yes, they're coming." His voice was deadpan, resigned in its shock at his failure to anticipate this turn of events and make good their escape to the hills. They all knew without anyone having to mention it that he of all people should have correctly predicted what course of action the Indonesian army would take. Meanwhile, her two brothers were up and about, dragging on items of clothing in a fit of panic.

"We've got to get out of here!" yelled Antonio.

"No!" her father barked back at him sharply. "Stay here!"

"You're crazy!" shouted Antonio. "Can't you hear those shells? They're coming in closer all the time."

"Of course I can hear them. Do you think we're going to be any safer from them out there in the street? Unless we receive a direct hit, we're better off inside. The walls will protect us from shrapnel blast. In a while the shelling will stop and then the town will be crawling with soldiers. The last thing we want is to be out and about when that happens. Now, everyone get under the table and let's pray none of those guns manage to find our roof."

"I can't stay here," said Antonio, not quite so loud this time but still in a voice shot through with panic.

"Do as you're told!" Francesca had never seen her father so decisive, so firm. It was as if, having let them down once with his wavering, he was determined to hold them together with his last reserves of resolve.

Antonio backed down, and together they pulled the table into the centre of the room, directly underneath the two largest beams, and covered it with blankets to shield them against flying glass. They stacked the sides with furniture to create something that to Francesca's eyes resembled a child's den. Her mother held the baby in her chest with one hand, comforting Marco with the other as they all clambered in to huddle together in their makeshift shelter. Around them, the shelling continued. It moved perilously closer so that Francesca thought it was only a matter of minutes before the blast waves whipped the flimsy walls and roof from around them to leave them naked to the street; and then it gradually moved away again. She knew that meant someone else was receiving a pounding and she was sorry for them, but all she really felt was a sense of relief that the barrage was no longer directly above their heads.

The baby, who up until then had done nothing more than shiver and whimper in her mother's arms, now began to howl. Her mother offered her her breast, but Angelica was too distraught to latch on properly. In the end, she rocked the baby to sleep with a gentle lullaby, which somehow also managed to soothe the rest of the family. Then the shelling diminished to the odd explosion in the distance, until it ceased altogether.

No one knew quite what to do. With the threat from artillery fire averted, temporarily at least, it seemed silly to remain under the table like children playing some Christmas party game. Francesca was curious to look outside, to see if any of the landmarks she knew so well had been destroyed. She wondered how her friends had fared, and Miguel too. Had their homes come under fire? Were they too, like themselves, crouched under some table terrified for their lives, or had they decided to run for it? Francesca wasn't entirely convinced as to the wisdom of her father's decision to stay put – her own instinct, like that of Antonio, was to grab what few essentials they could carry and make a dash for the countryside.

The lull, during which what was left of the night was given over to barking dogs and cockerels fenced in under hundreds of houses similar to theirs, didn't last long. They were out from under the table and beginning to ask themselves what they should do next when they heard the sound of aircraft approaching from the direction of the sea. First one or two, then dozens of them, droning so low overhead it seemed they would land on their rooftop.

"We've got to get out of here, father!" Antonio protested yet again. "They're coming in, they'll kill us all."

"No! The streets are far too dangerous. Anyone who's about will be shot for sure. We have to stay put."

"And do what?"

"Nothing. Just wait."

"For them to come here and take us away?"

"No, just wait for them to pass through. They're not interested in individual houses, it's the government buildings and radio station they'll want to secure. We can't do anything that risks getting in their way or we'll be dead for sure."

"I want to go," Antonio continued.

"And leave your family here?" Francesca watched her brother hesitate in the face of her father's words. "No, we're staying together through this as a family."

Antonio stood up and walked across to the front door, which he cracked open so he could peer through the narrow gap into the moonlight outside. Quickly he slammed it shut again, locking the door with the flimsy metal bolt.

"They're everywhere," he whispered, the blood draining from his face.

"Who?" asked her father.

"Parachutists. They're falling from the sky in thousands. That's what all those airplanes are doing."

"Oh, my God," her father said simply. "God help us now."

"We should have run when we had the chance." Antonio looked accusingly at their father, and from the way he evaded his son's gaze Francesca knew that he knew Antonio was right.

"Let me see," said Francesca all of a sudden, and before anyone could stop her she had crossed the room to the front window and lifted the blind to peep outside. All above, the sky was full of them, dotted figures like little toy soldiers dangling from the large circular parachutes by the neat, symmetrically arranged cords. She could just make out the rifles strapped tightly to each soldier's back, and the rope stretched from their legs to a large bag some ten feet below. Each time a paratrooper landed, the bag hitting the ground to announce his arrival a half second before the soldier kicked up a pile of dirt, rolled over and stood up again, running around into the wind to collapse the parachute, he was replaced by another two or three more spewing out of the open rear doorway of the large four-propeller aircraft. They were flying so low overhead she could make out the figure standing in the doorway giving out orders and throwing his charges into the void. Already the first troops were on the ground, and in the distance she heard the rat-a-tat-tat of small arms fire. After the artillery barrage it seemed almost harmless, chocolate gunfire from chocolate soldiers until it swung around in an arc to fly directly over their rooftop, where the deadly crack-crack-crack once again started up the chickens and the dogs.

Francesca dropped the blind back in place and rushed over to the bosom of her family, now huddled once again around the table. Her father was right, there really was no place for them to run now. All they could do was hope these soldiers from the sky were looking for something more significant than their little lives and would pass them by. She looked up at her mother, desperately trying to keep Angelica from crying. Francesca wished she would just shut up, she would draw attention to life inside their house. She wanted to put her hand over the baby girl's mouth, and momentarily she wondered that if it came to it, if they had to hide from the Indonesians as a family, would she be prepared to suffocate the baby to prevent her giving them all away? As if her mother could read her guilty thoughts, she pulled the infant closer still into her breast, where thankfully the crying receded into a whimper, for the time being at least.

While Antonio's fear was still shot through with rage at their father for keeping them in the house when they might have had a chance to make good their escape, Marco's terror was undiluted. He kept looking back and forth from one parent to the other, then to Francesca, on to his elder brother, even once to the baby. Gradually, the realization was dawning upon him – and Francesca's heart went out to him in the peeling-away of his innocence – that none of them could help him. How they had protected Marco, until recently the baby of the family himself, doing his homework, reassuring his nervous disposition, not letting him out of the house alone until a few short years ago… Here, now, when he really needed it, there was nothing any of them could do.

From outside, she could hear commands being barked out in Bahasa, interspersed with the sound of heavily laden boots clumping up and down the streets, together with more bursts of gunfire.

She fingered the silver crucifix around her neck and prayed. God, please help us now, she silently pleaded, please keep us safe from these soldiers, please help us, help us, just help us. God please, Jesus look after us, Mummy and Daddy and Antonio and Marco and baby Angelica, and me of course, please just keep us all safe, they can have whatever they want, just keep us safe from these terrible things happening outside.

The nuns at St. Xavier's had done a good job and her faith until then had been strong, but it evaporated in a crash of splintering wood, as the flimsy bolt on their own front door gave way to a vicious blow from a rifle butt. Her first thought was to wonder why her God had forsaken her, followed quickly by the realization that she had been conned by the nuns, and there was no God at all. Their reality was reduced to the four grinning Javanese soldiers now standing in their front room, rifles raised and pointing towards them.

———————

The story continues in *Francesca* by Donald Finnaeus Mayo.

# ECHOES

## Craig McDonald

### Author's note

My novel *Print the Legend* features novelist Hector Lassiter, variously known to the popular press as "the man who lives what he writes and writes what he lives," and as "the last man standing of the Lost Generation."

From the start of the Lassiter series, it was established Hector was fast friends with author Ernest Hemingway across many decades. The two rubbed shoulders as they worked to establish themselves as expatriate writers in 1920s Paris. *Print the Legend* turns on the legend of Hemingway, some of his notoriously lost early writings and the author's long persecution by the FBI under the directorship of J. Edgar Hoover.

The following *Print the Legend* excerpt finds Hector confronted with what appears to be a lost chapter of Papa's Paris memoir, *A Moveable Feast*, recalling a long-ago Christmas Eve in chilly Paris. As he reads along, Hector finds himself perplexed by the chapter's apparent overall authenticity, yet deeply troubled and even hurt by odd distortions potentially damaging to Hector's reputation and own "literary long game."

—Craig McDonald

Hector had ordered a bottle of Rioja Alta and he sat in the parlour of Suite 206, legs stretched out on the sofa and a big fire going. He had tuned the radio to a station that played only classical music. He lit a cigarette, sipped his wine and then carefully unfolded the copy of what was purported to be Hem's lost *A Moveable Feast* chapter and began to read…

### CHRISTMAS EVE AT LE SELECT MONTPARNASSE

It was another winter, the first since we had returned from Toronto, and money was even tighter than it had been the previous year and now it was Christmas Eve and I had not yet found a gift for my wife or for our child. Our money was mostly going for little chunks of charcoal or sometimes for some wood and for food for our baby. I was eating one meal a day so my wife could eat two. Because we were then very poor I had stayed away from writing in the cafés to save money and it had been several days, perhaps even a couple of weeks, since I had had a real drink.

I found Hector in Le Select, where we'd agreed the previous night to meet. It was just after ten and we'd both finished our mornings' writing. It was Christmas Eve and both of us being from the states, Christmas was still an important holiday for us. Hector was an only child from coastal Texas, so maybe Christmas was a little less important for him than for me. But only just a little.

I had grown up in the Midwest. There we had lived with seasons and Christmas was snow and family and a tree in the parlor. Christmas was gift exchanges and church services and the women of the family around the piano…a good fire and holiday food that always left one feeling too full and a little sick and perhaps even a little ashamed for having eaten too much.

I thought of the Christmases past that morning with Hector and thought I wouldn't have felt ashamed, at least not that morning, for having a too-full or at least even a full stomach.

"Lasso" was tall and slender and the one of us around the quarter whom Gertrude — whose authority on such matters one might be forgiven for doubting — insisted could have had a career in cinema with his "good looks and rich baritone" and "athletic bearing." He had a good smile and dimples and the palest blue eyes that would have been striking in a woman's face, or an actor's. But Hector was not a woman and he was not a cinema star (and some would say, not even a true or at least an honest writer, though some might later call him a credible actor).

But he was then a good and loyal friend and he was celebrating a book contract and so I could kid myself he was buying the drinks in celebration that morning and not treating me. Hector was writing for the crime pulp magazines back home, and making good money. Everyone called him a crime writer but he was really a writer who wrote stories with crime and the best of his stories might have fit well in a collection of stories such as "The Killers," if I had yet written that story. Or with many of Faulkner's short stories with criminal or rather crime elements.

But Hector was publishing his stories with some regularity then, and he had recently sold the first of his first fine crime novels. He had some money and he was thinking of moving out of the Quarter and perhaps even away from Paris. He spoke of perhaps going back home and to the Florida Keys where, he insisted, the living was even cheaper than in Paris and where it was so warm, all the time, that the houses didn't have fireplaces or even radiators.

In those days, Hector seemed always to be getting to the good and interesting places before me, or at least making a convincing case that he had. But Hector was a committed bachelor and I convinced myself that gave him certain critical advantages as an explorer. I'd first met Hector in Italy. He was driving ambulances after being injured and cashiered out and he trained me and taught me the tricks of driving the old rigs with their bankrupt, metal-on-metal brakes. Later, he'd been in Paris perhaps a year, or even two years before me, and, in this other case, he would beat me to Key West, too, though it might have been better for both of us if he had not.

But that was still many years away and this particular morning we were the best of friends and it was Christmas Eve and we were sitting by the fire and drinking belly-warming, tongue-loosening rum St. James. We sat on the terrace by the brazier and it was warmer there, but it was still a very cold morning, despite the sun, and we could see our breath as we talked and even see it a little when we breathed.

We spoke a bit of our morning's work and Hector told me he would be spending the holiday with a tart he'd met a few days before and whom he was trying to reform.

The girl's name was originally Victoria. She had come from St. Louis to Paris to be a singer or dancer.

But she had fallen through the layers of *bals musettes*, and then to the smaller *revues* in the poorest quarters, then into the *Folies Bergère* and finally had fallen further and now her working name was "Solange."

I'd met her once or twice and she was quite pretty with shining blue-black hair that she wore straight and long against fashion. Her eyes were blue, though not as blue as Hector's, and she had a pretty smile but she did not have dimples as Hector had. Still, she was quite pretty and one felt sad that she had come to Paris young and with dreams and had failed to meet those dreams, or even, really, to come close, and had come to debase herself as a streetwalker.

With his new money, Hector had recently moved her into his apartment, causing a small scandal with his haughty and newly religious *femme de ménage*, and so furthering his need of a new place to live.

"Vicky and I popped some corn this morning," Hector told me. "We spent the morning stringing the popcorn and after lunch we're going to go down to the Luxembourg gardens. I found a good pine tree there, like the Christmas trees from back home, and we'll string the popcorn around the tree and watch the birds eat the corn and we will drink some kirsch and sing a carol or two. You and your family should meet us there, Hem."

As if remembering then, Hector reached under the table to the empty chair next to him and fished around his overcoat's pocket. He handed me a small tissue-wrapped parcel and said, "Merry Christmas, Hem."

It was a metal flask and I could feel something sloshing inside it and was about to unscrew the lid to smell it when he said, "Pernod." He smiled and raised his rum St. James and said, "*Alla tue salute.*"

I said, "*Salud!*" and we toasted one another and then he handed me two other small parcels.

"The one in the red tissue is for Bumby," he said. "Some gizmo I saw the other day." The other, he said, was for my wife. Hector was just a bit younger than me, and my wife treated Hector like a kid brother most of the time. But sometimes they would flirt with one another and I knew they were quite fond of one another and that Hector perhaps even had a kind of crush on my wife. That is, if a man like Hector could be said to have "crushes." But it was all very innocent that time, and when I had still been working as a journalist, and would sometimes be away on assignment, I knew Hector would watch out for her, and for our son, and that they were safe together and that nothing untoward would happen.

But now I could feel the contours of the gift through the tissue and I could feel the anger building in me. My wife's red hair was growing out raggedly and thick after the baby and she had lost one of her fine hair brushes in the move back from Toronto. Just that morning, as I was leaving, she had been cursing the tangles in her thick red hair.

We had been out with Hector and his reformed tart a few nights before and my wife had seen an antique, silver brush in the window of a shop and had commented on it. I knew the present must be the brush that she had admired.

"I can't accept this, Lasso," I said.

"It's not for you, Hem," Hector said carefully. "Tell her it's from you. You should do that anyway. Anything else might look…improper." He gave me his best smile then, or what I knew to be what he thought was his best smile; his boyish, winning smile with dimples that could erase any slight or injury, or so he clearly thought. Often enough he was right. And my first drinks in several weeks had left me mellow and warm.

But it still wasn't working all the way upon me yet, and sensing that, Hector said, "You two are the closest thing to family I have, Hem, and it's Christmas and that's about the giving. You'll just have to live with the receiving, you righteous son of a bitch." He pointed to the gift for our son. "I've got no brother or sisters, so I'll never have nieces or nephews, either. I'm afraid Bumby fulfills that need for me. Christ, Hem, please let me have my Christmas. Without it, I'm left to decorating trees in the gardens with fallen women. What kind of Yule is that? You can't appreciate family, truly, when you have one. When you don't, it's all you think about."

I still wasn't completely soothed or convinced, but I was then terribly fond of Hector. I didn't yet know what I would do with the gifts, and, if I took them home, what I would say about their origins, but his smile and steady blue-eyed gaze broke down the last of my resentment and jealously and my guilt for having no money.

We toasted one another again and I tried to think of something I might have around our small apartment to give Hector as a gift.

Hector ordered us both Welsh 'Rarebit' and we sipped more of our rum and I said, "What did you get Vicky for Christmas?"

Hector shook his head and then shook loose a cigarette and struck a match with his thumbnail and lit his cigarette.

He stared into the coal fire of the brazier.

Finally he sighed and said, "An abortion."

Hector sighed and bit his lip and sipped more wine. Hem's sketch of that long-gone Christmas Eve was accurate, and it *wasn't*.

---

The story continues in *Print the Legend* by Craig McDonald.

# SO BE GOOD FOR GOODNESS SAKE

## Colin O'Sullivan

Colin O'Sullivan is the author of *Killarney Blues*, a terse, pulsing Irish drama. Writer Niall Griffiths said about *Killarney Blues*: "Colin O'Sullivan writes with a style and a swagger all his own. His voice - unique, strong, startlingly expressive - both comes from and adds to Ireland's long and lovely literary lineage. Like many of that island's sons and daughters, O'Sullivan sends language out on a gleeful spree, exuberant, defiant, ever-ready for a party. Only a soul of stone could resist joining in."

*So Be Good for Goodness Sake* is also set in O'Sullivan's native Kerry, though the location of O'Laughlin's field is fictitious.

---

*Straw faces, long faces, eyes, where are the eyes in the straw faces, long faces? The music doesn't stop; it just gets louder and faster, faster and louder. The mummers dance, look at them go, round and round, heel to the toe, the tin instruments clash and clang, what are they but made of tin and can, and the mummers take partners by the hand, and it's more of this twirling and writhing round the bonfire fast as cancan as the sparks fly and more logs are thrown on to help its crackle and hiss and the audience claps along to the trilling band.*

*They dance until they're weary. They have drunk and drunk from the necks of black bottles and they are tired and inebriated and yet not retiring. Still they go. Still they go, round and round, heel to the toe. Look at them, look at them, take your hand away from your face and look at them, don't be scared. Don't be frightened of these straw men, these long-faced men. There are worse things, there are worse things in the world; they're just men, men dancing, mummers, just men though, aren't they, underneath the strange apparel? Just men, with men's desires, round they go, heel to the toe.*

The knife slices through the flesh. The carver is not holding back, he slices clean with a stiff and sturdy hand. The meat folds and falls softly to the plates and the hungry cannot take their eyes off it. The carver takes pride in his action, been doing this for years, and has never yet messed it up. The turkeys are always top of the range and the hungry are always satisfied. That's what tradition means to John Harty, and although he moans about not being around to see another one, here he is, presiding over another Christmas dinner in the afternoon, knife brandished, and the fine fat bird on the table getting ripped apart for his guests.

"And to think some poor sods are actually vegetarian," he says.

"I know, the poor things. Slice off some of the dark meat for me, John," says Mary Doolan, winking at Anita across the table. "I like the dark stuff."

Anita is trying to enjoy herself. She's been away so long that she is not used to the customs, unused to the give and take, the blather; it's her first Christmas back, and friends and family have welcomed her and have lain this feast in front of her; her good uncle John, head of the party, eager to begin life again after the sad passing of his wife, is eager to show off the seventy-year-old but sprightly new bride, Mary. Cousin Tony is there too, Tall Tony, knocking back the bottles of beer that he brought for the occasion, knocking 'em back like there is no tomorrow. Anita is hoping there really is no tomorrow. Harry and his wife Maureen are there too, and their eighteen-year-old, Melinda, or is it Malinda, who everyone calls Missy, to her chagrin, slouched and moody, probably wishing she were anywhere else. It is Christmas Day and they are having Christmas dinner, and Anita is trying her best to enjoy herself, trying to acclimatise. But the dreams keep coming back to her, the nightmares, the flashbacks, she doesn't even have to be asleep, all she needs to do is stare blankly at the wall or the ceiling and the images play there, again, and again. It was this time, this holiday season, all those years ago. Anita watches the carving of the meat and notices how sharp the knife is and her skin tingles.

*The smell is of straw and trampled grass, a circus smell, and the smoke in the winter air, is that a whiff of the Devil himself or it is just a strand of straw taking light?*

*It's dangerous if you step too close.*

*It's dangerous in the dark and if you step too close.*

The ceiling plays it all.

*Louder. Faster. Faster louder. It makes the head spin. And they keep going. They do not stop, these mummers, no matter how weary, no matter how drunk. It seems like they will never stop.*

*Take your hand away from your face and look at them, don't be frightened. Look at them look at them look at them!*

"Are you all right, Anita dear? You look like you are miles away."

"Oh, I'm fine — just not used to drinking, I suppose."

She has hardly touched a drop of the white wine in front of her. But it will do as an excuse. She has heard that the other uncle, Donal, might turn up today, and he is sure to be there leading the parade tomorrow, and for that reason she quivers.

Jokes continue around the table; at least the other three seem to be enjoying themselves; John rolls his eyes at everything Mary says but everyone can see quite clearly that he is glad to have her around, he's a new man. She brings a comic bluster to the party: Anita knows this after only a second meeting, and she is glad to be placed next to her; good company, normal people, an experience she hasn't had for such a long time; good company, yes, even if it is in the form of an old dame with a bottomless bucket of bawdy banter and endless tease.

As if to illustrate such characteristics Mary lets rip with another typically salacious comment:

"Now, put that knife down Johnny and let me give your cracker a good pull."

"It was only a matter of time," says Tony. "And she hasn't even started drinking yet!"

Anita ignores the ceiling and tries to make herself laugh.

Not long ago she would have reached for a cigarette. That feeling of being full to the brim, feeling like you are about to burst, that was the time she always enjoyed sparking up a Marlboro Light and blowing streams of grey smoke contentedly to the air. She was allowed smoke in the hospital, in the day room at least. It gave the patients something to do. But smoking is another thing she has left behind. She has moved on. She has gotten clean. She doesn't do drugs anymore. She is fresh and new – if old John Harty can be a new man at seventy-two, then she can be a new woman at forty – and at this moment she can hardly move a muscle for the sheer volume of food she has shoved into her face over the last couple of hours.

Her companions appear to be in the same bloat. They may never rise from this table again. They are so full that they could happily just sit here, and slowly expire, their last supper indeed a pleasant one.

Anita is doing her best to enjoy herself, and now she desperately needs to go to the toilet. She cannot bring herself to move though. She'll wait it out a few minutes longer.

Mary proposes a song, a *sing-song* as she puts it, and a few more crackers to pull in the hope that the jokes might be good. But everyone knows the jokes are never good in Christmas crackers and so she has no takers.

*With the blindfold on she cannot tell how many there are. These are male voices that spin around her. These are jeering voices, loud voices, drunk voices. Where are Irene and Fiona and Laura? Her friends. Where are they? They were there one minute, next they are gone. Could they have got burned up in the bonfire? Could these men have thrown them on the fire and watched them go up in flames? No, no, she didn't hear any screams; she would have heard screams for sure. Her ears still work, her eyes are blocked, yes, but her ears are working fine, she still hears the gruff male voices, singing loud, dancing, their heavy boots thumping on the field, flattening the grass even more, and dancing too, weaving in and out to the tin can music, the tin whistles, the jigs, the polkas — she does not know the difference between a jig and a polka, never learned that stuff, all she ever wanted in these first seventeen years of her life was to waltz, to waltz with a fine young*

*handsome man, to learn it properly; that is about all she knows*
*about romance, a waltz, something gleamed from a child's book,*
*Cinderella maybe, a prince leading the golden girl around the*
*ballroom, something silly, jejune.*

"Tomorrow the wren boys will be out and about, it might
be worth a look. We could go and see that. It's been years
since I've seen them at it. 'Twas a lot more popular when I was
young. It was a good laugh, seeing all them dressed up and
dancing about," says Mary.

Anita looks down at her glass. The wine has gone and now
she has this sloe drink. She remembers it from the past. It was
there then, too.

*It's dangerous if you step too close to the fire, he tells her, step*
*away, let me take you away.*

"Not a bad idea," says Tony. "I've never seen them, ever,
as far as I know."

"That's because you spent most of your youth in towns
and cities," says his Uncle John. "This is a country thing. Your
mother and father used to enjoy it too, Anita, God rest 'em,
but... I'm sure we don't need to be out in the cold watching
that old nonsense. Not at my age anyway."

"I'm not even sure what it's all about. How it started I
mean. So, who's going to explain it to me?" says Tony.

Anita gets up and leaves the room, it's about time she vis-
ited the toilet; she cannot hold it in any longer.

Mary decides to educate Tall Tony:

"The biggest one in Kerry might be the Dingle one I
suppose, only a few villages around here still do it. And I
know that just outside the town, in O'Laughlin's field, they
have a bonfire, they do it every year, have been at it since I
was a girl."

"A long, long time ago," says John, but Mary ignores the jibe, continuing her explanation.

"The wren, or *wran*, as it is often pronounced, is a bird, as you know, and the tradition is all about hunting this wren, a fake one now, which they put on top of a pole. Then the men, all dressed up in straw outfits, masks and stuff, have a parade through the town and play music, fiddles and things, you know. It's an old tradition."

John helps expand the story:

"The reason they celebrate the wren, a fella in a bar once told me, is that the bird is known for singing even in mid-winter, when a lot of other birds are cold and silent. The wren keeps going. Sometimes they even call the bird *Winter Wren*. Cahersiveen is a strong place for it, that's what the song that "The Boys of Barr na Sráide" is about. The song tells of the *dreolín*. That's Irish for *wren*. Ivy ruler. You see Tony, you could learn a thing or two here. About your own parishes."

"Yes, a history and culture lesson wrapped in one, how lucky I am to be surrounded by such wisdom."

Mary begins to darken the tale however by adding that:

"Not all of it is fun, those wrenboys, you know, there was a story going round about them being up to all kinds of terrible things. The masks were licence to get up to all sorts of devilment. This is going back a bit mind, twenty odd years ago. And they'd be loaded up on poteen... there was a story of some young one getting hurt if I can recall, but apparently there must be Guards present at these events now, in case of any accidents, you know how it is."

In the bathroom Anita is looking at herself in the mirror. *The wren the wren the king of all birds*, she says slowly to herself. Her face has grown ashen, the colour drained from her. Can she deal with it? If they are to go, if they are to actually make it there to that field... can she handle it? Can she look into the faces, those long straw faces, and can she bear it? She'll need a lot more liquid courage to get up there. But she *has to*. She *must* go there. Because if she doesn't go there and face her demon, how then is she ever to sleep?

*They have put a blindfold on her so that she cannot see their faces. One of them tells her it is a game, a game for the twenty-sixth, an old traditional game. She hears the joke in his voice and it must be true, maybe they do play games on the twenty-sixth of December, like they play at other times of the year, like Halloween. This day, yes, this day must be just like Halloween. Nothing to be frightened of then, the ghouls aren't real, only masks. She doesn't not know why one of these young men has suggested she wear a blindfold, because she can't see their faces anyway, the hidden faces of these straw men, these long faces with their mad chants and hell of a din. At the moment all she can see is the orange glow from the fire, everything else behind the blindfold, everything else is just shadow and blur.*

She takes a deep breath and then makes her way back to the living room, smiling. It's a false smile, like the wren atop the pole, fake, for show, but it'll have to do. As breezily as she can, she says:

"Well, have we planned our activities? Not doing a pub quiz or anything, I hope. I'm not sure I'm so well up on my general knowledge these days."

She wonders if they know all about her. Her history. Why she was inside for so long, why she was taken away, put into care. John does. He knows. Benevolent Uncle John. Not like her other uncle, who might very well be leading the mummers as he has done almost every year. The king of them. Has John told the others? Can they see it in her eyes?

"We've decided, we're all going to see the Wrenboys' bonfire tomorrow," says Mary.

Anita shows no sign of displeasure. She leans on the wall to keep herself steady. So she'll be in O'Laughlin's field again, at the fire again, facing the fear again. She is new; she can handle it.

"Sounds like fun," says Anita. "Maybe I'll bring a bottle of this for them. Keep their spirits up while they're entertaining us with their mummery."

She holds up the bottle of sloe gin that John has made.

"If there'll be any left," says John. "Look at the way Mary is tucking into it."

Mary Doolan makes a play of taking a big gulp from the neck of the bottle. Some of it drips down her chin as she breaks into laughter and John pushes a box of tissues in her direction.

"Mary, what'll we do with you? Can't take you anywhere."

Anita wakes with a slight headache, but nothing that a good strong coffee can't fix. She needs to be fresh today. She has a lot to think about.

*It's dangerous if you step too close to the fire, he tells her, step away, let me take you away.*

Don't. Don't let the dreams in. Even as they try to make their way, their incessant burrowing, stop them. Everything will come together today. This is it. She needs to sleep at night. She needs to kill the nightmares.

At home she puts her legs up and is resting. She needs this time to relax. She needs an hour or two before they all get together, before the trip to O'Laughlin's field. She has eaten breakfast and now has enough time for some delicate sounds on her stereo, the relaxation CDs she used for meditation in the clinic. Morning has gone. It is slipping into afternoon. She is in her bedroom. The quiet CD of waterfalls and whales has stopped, and suddenly it grows loud and raucous.

*Faster and louder. The mummers dance, but she can't see them go round and round, heel to the toe. The heat of the bonfire is on her face so she must be close to it. She is scared now, it doesn't feel so "gamey" anymore, feels like she might be stepping over the line, some line, some line she might be crossing over, or a river say, the River Styx. Her heart beats faster.*

*Fiona! She calls.*

*Fiona doesn't answer.*

*Maura!*

*Maura doesn't answer.*

*Irene!*

*Ditto.*

*They say that word in school, the girls, "ditto"; they heard some Americans say it on a TV show. A funny word, they love the sound of it and they smile cheeky smiles when they say it to each other in the school corridors, or when copying homework from each other.*

*Keep it together girl, she says to herself, your friends are gone, or they are hiding, it's just a game, don't be scared of these straw men, these long-faced men. There are worse things, there are worse things in the world, these are just men, men dancing, mummers, having fun, just men though, aren't they? Just men, with men's desires, round they go, heel to the toe.*

The team assembles then in the late afternoon as the clouds loom. It might rain. It probably will. But it won't stop them from going to see the Wren Boys.

They have buttoned up their coats, put wooly hats upon their heads and have tied scarves around their necks. It will be cold in this field, no matter how close to the bonfire they get. It will be cold. December in Kerry. The end of the year. The end of…

They pile into his surprisingly small car, Mary making quips about the lanky legs of the driver and how a bigger car would be more suitable.

"Thank God it's only a short journey," says John Harty as they make their way to the countryside.

The rain is holding off and the visitors are glad of this. No pour yet. They leave the car and tread carefully on the grass. Anita continues her mini-quakes; she feels the land could give way underneath her at any moment, as if the whole damn expanse could open up and greedily swallow, drag her all the way down to Hades.

Already a small crowd has gathered for the festivities: families, mothers and fathers holding the hands of their giddy offspring, still warm from the glow of Santa and his magic; all these comfortable souls, willing to take part in this ancient rite; it's an education. It's an education for Anita and Tony as well as for those kids. Maybe it's a connection too, to older ways, and like John's sloe gin might make her feel part of the earth, closer to the land… unless of course again she will be forced to leave and enter the abyss of herself. She may well.

Someone starts with a match, brings match to torch, brings torch to pyre, and soon there is smoke and soon flame. The flames are quickly dancing and all they have to do now is wait for the human dancers to come, human dancers in masquerade.

A great cheer resounds when they do arrive, the peculiar mummers, led by a fake wooden hobbyhorse-like contraption. This is a curious piece of work, like an *objet* from some grim apocalyptic art exhibition, a Goya scene come monstrously to life say, or a Guernica extra; it's all head and swinging mouth, this beastly construction, a rocking horse gone off its rocker.

The mummers have begun their chants and incantations, and the music soon erupts, tin whistles and fiddles and the crashings of small cymbals. The children's faces show expressions mixed: fascination and terror. They cling to their parents, holding hands tighter, little fingers clasped around bigger, stronger ones, not letting go. Maybe deep down they know that these are just men dressed up, but still, still, how can they ever be sure, of anything? Many of them thought Santa Claus came yesterday with a sack full of goodies, and many of them think that a heavenly father is watching down on them and that Hell exists, too, and is way down there beneath them, where they desperately do not want to end up. So be good for goodness sake.

Anita watches the mummers too, like a child, fascination and terror, and grim remembrance. This is where it had happened. And this is where something is happening now.

*The smell is of straw and trampled grass, a circus smell, and the smoke in the winter air, is that a whiff of the Devil or it is just a strand of straw taking light?*

*And is that the voice of the Devil too?*

She can see a smaller member. A smaller, masked hunter, all skips and sways, out of time to the music but charging forward to the bonfire nonetheless, eyes peering out through holes, watching the wren on top of the pole.

That must be Marcus, Anita thinks, Donal's son, her own cousin, she has heard about the boy, a fourteen-year-old, a chip off the old block. He follows his father of course, that must be him, Uncle Donal, for although she cannot see his eyes, Anita knows the dark cold stare is there, behind the straw cover, intent and focused on the event. That's Donal Harty leading the way all right, and his cohorts in tow. And look at the mad horsehead snapping, biting at the air. Goya? Guernica? Just grotesque.

Anita's nerves are a jangle, also out of time with the music, and the sounds carry on the air in waves, aural peaks and troughs.

They all convene around the bonfire. Anita seems to remember that there was more than one back then, maybe three, even four bonfires, rejoices of flame to the night sky, but they have only one now. A Guard keeps watch over the whole event, making sure no one gets too close to the fire, making sure children are kept well back, making sure that the mummers dance and play and that is all they do, for there have been tales from the past, old rumours or old wives tales or old gossip or mere fabrication, who knows, but still and all, keep an eye, keep an eye, that way it's all just a bit of fun.

*It's dangerous if you step too close.*

*It's dangerous in the dark and if you step too close.*

The crowd has started to clap and cheer. And the mummers respond terrifically, their jumps higher, their shouts more boisterous, more booming.

Anita watches it all and grows uncomfortable. She turns to her friends and asks them if they too feel the cold descending on them, and they nod and Tony exaggerates chattering teeth. It is the right time to take a bottle of sloe gin from her backpack.

"You sneaky old devil," says John Harty, delighted to uncork it with his trusty Swiss army knife, and delighted too to take the first sip.

"Perhaps we could offer it to the dancers," says Tony, not sure what to call these ghoulish performers.

"That's what I was thinking too," says Anita. "Exactly what I was thinking. That's why I brought extra."

The little boy is staring at her now. Whatever she has said, or whatever he has picked up on, even from a distance, he has turned his sights on her. He stares. He doesn't take his eyes off her. Does he recognise her? How could he? They have never met. She had been inside. But he doesn't take his eyes off her. And that's all she can see, eyes, because the rest of the face and body are covered. Eyes. Only eyes. Anita's knees are almost knocking, such is the fear running through her, the cold, the fear and the remembrance.

*Come with me, he says, step right this way.*

*Like it's a circus, yes, like it's a game and she's about to go through some looking-glass and appear at some dandy carnival on the other side and maybe the young gent will lead her on a wonderful waltz.*

He had taken her from the field that day, led her by the hand like she was a child. She had followed his mesmeric tones, like she was in a trance, like she was hypnotized by him. She was not drunk. She was just fooled. Foolish and fooled. Gullible. Young.

*Come with me.*

She did.

She had known his voice? A trusted voice. She had known, hadn't she?

He had held her hand softly at first but as they walked away from friends and festivities he increased his hold on her, squeezing her fingers, tugging her along. She had laughed for the first part of their walk but as they moved further along the thick grass and away from the flames she began to tremble, as if she was moving away from the warmth of the sun and out into deep, black, cold space, the other side of the galaxy, her fear increasing with every step.

The youth, Marcus, walks towards them, towards Anita who walks towards his father who has stopped by the fire and is taking a small break. Donal Harty has stopped dancing because he is tired. When he was younger he had strength and vigour and selfish power, but now that he is sixty he is getting tired.

He must be sixty now – did he have the boy late? – and how old was he back then? Thirty-seven. Twenty years older than she was.

The others keep dancing but Donal Harty is taking a time-out. The music for once is too loud for him, even his own bodhrán that he has brought along to beat, even that now too is bothersome. The chaos around him is getting too much, he'll need to retire, hand over the reins to his boy. His time must surely be up. He's glad his son is there today; a rite of passage, becoming a man, and look at his eyes in that mask, the same piercing eyes as himself: it's like looking in a mirror.

She had followed him and knew, maybe even knew then that something bad was going to happen. It was no waltz. On she went with him, to where a lone car was parked. Did he own a car then? The door was open; he just pulled her into the back seat. He was rough then, rough and pulling at her.

His smile was gone, his attempts at humour and jokes gone, the charm at family get-togethers, Christmas parties — was there even charm in the first place, or had she created it? – all vanished.

He was on top of her then and she didn't even know how to scream.

The trio has moved towards the bonfire from three different directions. The heat rages between them and Anita keeps shuffling towards the man behind the mask.

Then Anita is suddenly before Donal. This is the man. Her uncle. These are the eyes of him, eyes behind the mask.

He straightens up to look at her, face to face, real face to covered face.

"Anita," he says, taking off his mask

He turns to the boy, nervously, "Marcus, this is a cousin of yours."

The boy says nothing, just takes off his mask too and looks up at her. He is small for his age, lacking the bulk of his father. He looks younger than he actually is, his thin frame, his smooth skin, but his eyes look old, ancient.

She is doing her best to force a smile, but her hands shake, her knees still jelly.

"So you are back," says Donal.

"I am," she says.

She lay on the back seat. Her first time. This was about as romantic as the world got. Her first time. No waltz. Just a heaving man, smelling of bonfire smoke and Major cigarettes and alcohol. How did she let all that happen? Did she struggle against him? Where was her fight? Because she wanted it. That's what he had kept saying to her, growling at her: *you want it, don't say you don't want it, I could see it in your eyes across the field. You're just as much a whore as the others.*

Where were her friends? Would they look for her? Maybe they just saw her going off with her uncle, and sure, what harm in that?

She doesn't know what to say to him now. And Donal looks just as confused as he stares at her, his eyes trying not to meet hers.

But here she is, clutching her backpack in her sweaty hand, and in that bag are bottles of sloe gin, one she has laced with all the pills she took with her from the clinic, ones that calmed her down when she was agitated, when she was coming off the hard drugs. They are all mixed in that bottle of sloe gin now, swirling and poisonous, ruinous.

He had gin that day, Donal. That day in the car he had reached under the driver's seat and pulled out a bottle of purple sloe gin. It was dark like wine, but it wasn't wine, no, darker. He told her to drink it, and to loosen up a bit. So she drank it. She thought it bitter and didn't like it one bit but she swallowed it anyway. He guzzled it down. He wanted her to drink more because then she wouldn't feel so tight and he could try at her again. So she drank more and he lay on her again and this time he had his own trousers down and he was taking her hand and putting it on him and she could feel his hardness and she was terrified. She knew she would have to do it sometime, she may have even been late starting, the others had surely done it, at least they had said they had, but she didn't want it like this, not rough and reeking and unplanned and with a man she was supposed to trust. Why was she not fighting? Why was she so dead? He put his hands on her throat and told her to loosen up, that she was getting it whether she like liked it or not, and when still she was closing and not opening and being difficult and unresponsive, that's when he pulled out the knife, and he looked too shocked and unsure of himself to use it, but there it was, sticking out, like his own penis, sticking grotesquely out at her, the knife hard and wanting flesh to cut, his cock swollen and unsatisfied, so he pushed himself into her, the knife beside them on the seat, and he heaved and heaved and thrust and pushed and it felt wickedly painful, this stabbing into her, and that's when her moans started to get louder, turning into screams, but somehow the screams weren't coming out, were like silent screams, is there such a thing? For no one heard a sound. He was telling her that he was going to come in a minute and not to be such a little bitch, that he was her uncle and family members did favours for each other, but she just trembled and buckled and cried, because she knew she wasn't a bitch, and family members did not do these kind of favours, it's just that this was all wrong and she needed him to stop it, it hurt, and that's when he picked up the knife and…maybe he only meant to threaten her, to frighten her further into compliance, but his control was restricted, being stuck inside her, and his swinging arm was foolishly fast and he sliced down the side of her breast where he had forced open her shirt and bra and suddenly there was blood, a spatter of it on his face, and the sudden pulling out of her body made him ejaculate on top of her, and that's the first time she saw ever saw sperm, wet and thick and white and useless on her own flesh, and soon there was a flow of blood mixing with it into an ugly pink and the terror of it made her scream only silence again, like when they suddenly turn off the sound in a movie, nothing coming out, only a terrific void, and Donal stumbled out of the car and threw up a purple mess on the lonely dirt road, as if there hadn't been enough emissions of colour that terrible afternoon.

"You probably need a drink," she says to him as she hands him the bottle.

"Wow, I haven't seen a bottle of sloe gin in a long time, where did you get it?"

"Your brother made it."

"Very impressive," he says as he swigs from the neck. "God, but that takes me back."

Anita is downcast, suddenly down. He is there drinking from the bottle and she had a choice, and she took it, and now he drinks from it, and she watches him and he nods his appreciation and she tells him to drink up and hopes it takes him back, and then she walks away from them. Just walks away. The music has stopped: the mummers mummed.

No sound.

Anita's movie silence is like a continuation of what it was back then; she must ask someone to turn the sound back on. Even the tinny music is better than its alarming absence. Anita stops and has to decide quickly. Stay or go. The plan was to go.

Tony's face could be that in a Munch painting, horror-struck, terrified, and he is running now, to where Donal Harty has collapsed on the ground; all of a sudden, he just collapsed, right there in front of them, and Mary and John kneel over him, clutching his hand. Is this man having a heart attack? Uncle. Uncle Donal. Is he about to expire right here in this place of dreadful drama and depravity?

When they turn around to find her, she is nowhere to be seen, because Anita has already set off across the grass and into the waiting taxi, the one she had ordered hours ago. And she doesn't look back at the field where her friends searched, Irene and Fiona and Maura all those years ago, and her friends now search, Tony, John and Mary, and she doesn't look back to see the teenage boy go to his father lying on the ground, clutching his chest, and she doesn't care that the tin can music begins its merriment again, and she doesn't wait to see the rain start up its drizzle, then its pelt, and hear the groans from the players, and the rain beats down harder on the emptying field, the grass trampled and the dark soil soon sludgy, and the clouds in anger decide to punish the place, and the thunder barks like hungry hellish hounds let loose on some wanton world.

# THE RETURN OF EDDIE SLOAN

## Kevin Stevens

Kevin Stevens is the author of *Reach the Shining River*, "not only a solid murder mystery, but equally a colourful and thought-provoking study of a moment in time. With the rhythm and cadence of the prose, echoing the blues soundtrack that underscored the whole book, Stevens easily achieved that balance between crime fiction and literary fiction due to his exceptional characterization and engaging prose." —*Raven Crime Reads*

The following story is set in Kansas City in 1935, after the events described in the novel.

———————

She woke, thirsty and scared. A man stood in the doorway of her bedroom. She saw the glow of his cigarette coal, the outline of his porkpie hat.

"Hello, Arlene," he said.

His voice went through her body like forked lightning.

"Eddie," she whispered.

He dropped the cigarette to the floor and ground it with his heel. "I told you I'd be back."

She gulped for air, leaned toward the nightstand, and clicked on the light.

The doorway was empty.

She rose from bed and went into the kitchen. Moonlight blued the floorboards. The woodstove was cold, the window panes pale with frost. Her breath froze into hazy clouds, but her hands were clammy with sweat.

She checked on Wardell. He was fast asleep, dreaming of sugar plums. All the doors were locked. The backyard was deserted and the thin cover of fresh snow showed no footprints. In the parlor, the Christmas tree stood lightless and lonely, the angel on top askew. She pulled her robe tight around her shoulders and returned to bed. Passing the threshold, she examined the smudge of ash on the pinewood floor. It was in the shape of a heart.

Eddie had been dead for over four months. On their last night together they had argued, bitterly. She had wanted him to stay with her. *I'm not inclined*, he had said. She told him angrily to go to his friends. *See if I care*, she said. Her last words to him. Words that hung in eternity like stars. Words that were burned into her heart. How could she have known that he was working for the wrong men? That he was in mortal danger? That she would never see him again?

*I'll be back.* Yes, he had said that during the long argument. But what else would she have thought except that he would come to her the next day? A day he would never see.

After Wardell had come home from school and she had fed him fried chicken and white gravy and he did his homework and Leonora, her friend from church, had come over to babysit, Arlene put on her blue dress, the shimmering one with sequins and bows, and took the streetcar to the club. It was the Friday before Christmas. Expecting a big crowd, Piney had promised her a twenty-dollar bonus. Through the frosted car window the stores were open late and the streets were festooned with colored lights. The bundled figures of passers-by, carrying boxes of gifts and bags of groceries, moved like ghosts.

She got off on Vine Street and hustled into the Gaslight Club, where Piney fed her ribs and greens and Phineas Jordan warmed her up on the battered piano and Sam the barkeep smiled his warm smile as he poured her bourbon. She was smoking again and had suffered a series of colds this winter, so her voice was tired and a little ragged. But Piney told her it gave her singing a new edge, rich and bluesy, and she had added several new songs to her repertoire – *Gin House Blues* and *Careless Love* and *I Need a Little Sugar in My Bowl*. And for tonight, her own versions of *Silent Night* and *The First Noël*.

"You doin' all right?" Piney said, looking into her eyes.

"Yes, Piney, I'm doing fine."

"Touch of fever maybe?"

She patted his shoulder. "Get the people in. I'm ready."

Slowly, in pairs and small groups, the locals arrived, shedding their winter coats to reveal zoot suits and satin evening dresses, ordering cocktails and bantering with Sam. She recognized most of them from church socials or the district stores. Locals. The business trade and city folk stayed away as the holidays approached. Tonight was a Friday night crowd, all the more festive for the holiday season. Ready to unzip. Ready to dance.

Arlene went into the dressing room for the final few minutes before the show. It was part of her routine: she slowed her breathing and thought about the first song, imagining herself inside the words and music. For several months after Eddie's death she had sung for him. She thought it would make her feel better, but the opposite had happened. Grief could not last forever, and as Christmas approached and Wardell grew excited about Santa Claus, she knew it was time to move on. Her man was gone. Her son should be her focus now. So she had concentrated on her technique and her choice of songs, working with Phineas to make sure the show gave the patrons their money's worth. Making sure she made the living that would support Wardell.

She took the stage, and the crowd murmured their approval. They knew her. They liked her. Piney had placed another bourbon on the piano and she sipped as Phineas played the intro to *Lover Come Back to Me*. Stepping into the footlights, she began singing.

*You came at last*
*Love had its day*
*That day is past*
*You've gone away*
*This aching heart of mine is singing*
*Lover come back to me*

The song led her on, but as the bourbon warmed her blood and the crowd loosened and responded, church-style, something was different. The image of Eddie in the doorway would not leave her. His silhouette was like a holy picture in her mind's eye, a saint's portrait hung to remind her that this was a sacred time of year, a time of forgiveness and rebirth. And as the song neared its end, she decided not to resist but to go with the vision, and she closed her eyes and sang with rare emotion, the feelings of the last year welling up in her, flooding through her, and it was all she could do to keep her voice steady. And while she sang, a smaller voice inside her spoke, one that only she could hear, saying, "I love you, Eddie. I will never forget you."

As the song closed, the audience recognized that they had heard something rare and powerful. And at the beginning of a set, when most performers were only getting warmed up! They stood and applauded heartily and shouted for more. She opened her eyes and she saw, through a blur of tears, her friends and neighbors clapping with great spirit, their own faces filled with something like the blessed feeling that had come to her as if from heaven.

She looked at Phineas, who was grinning and nodding, and Piney, who gave her a thumbs up, and as she wiped her eyes and reached for the bourbon, she saw Eddie at the back of the club. He sat on a high stool, nursing a double whiskey as he had always done when he came to hear her, his hat at an angle, his lips set in a wry smile. Across the crowded room her eyes locked onto his and everything went quiet and a bright peace filled her soul. Because his eyes were saying to her: "I know you care. I will always be here."

She smiled back as he lifted his glass. Then she nodded at Phineas and he counted off the next tune. And she sang.

*My heart is sad and lonely*
*For you, I sigh, for you, dear only*
*Why haven't you seen it, I'm all for you*
*Body and soul..."*

———————

Read Arlene's story in *Reach the Shining River* by Kevin Stevens.

# ABOUT THE AUTHORS

**Hadley Colt** is the author of *Permanent Fatal Error*, published by Betimes Books in 2014.

The name is the pseudonym for an internationally acclaimed author. Hadley Colt's previous novels were published in several languages to excellent reviews and high praise from fellow writers who've declared the author's work *"non conformist"*, *"bold and extravagant"*, *"an explosive mix of humor and action"*, and who has been described as *"an erudite with formidable imagination"* and a *"master of suspense"*.

**Sam Hawken** is the author of *La Frontera*, published by Betimes Books in 2013.

His first novel, *The Dead Women of Juarez* was published in the UK, France and Germany and shortlisted for the CWA "New Blood" Dagger Award 2011. He is also the author of *Tequila Sunset* (nominated for the Gold Dagger 2013), *Missing* and of a number of short stories. Sam Hawken's fiction embraces a broad spectrum of genres and involves extensive research, authentic flavour, and a devotion to dealing with issues both historical and contemporary.

**David Hogan** is the author of *The Last Island*, published by Betimes Books in 2013.

He is also an acclaimed playwright whose works have been widely produced. Most recently, the NPI-award winning *Capital* was recommended by LA Weekly and *No Sit – No Stand – No Lie* opened the 'Resilience of the Spirit' Human Rights Festival in San Diego, California. A dual citizen of the US and Ireland, David Hogan lived and worked in Greece for a number of years. He currently resides in Southern California.

**Richard Kalich** is the author of *Central Park West Trilogy: The Nihilesthete, Penthouse F, Charlie P*, published by Betimes Books in 2014.

Kalich was born in New York and grew up on the Upper West side, where he still resides. His novels have been published in Bulgaria, Denmark, England, Germany, Holland, Israel, Russia, Sweden, Turkey and Japan to critical acclaim.

"Kalich is a successful novelist, one who has succeeded in consistently producing perplexing fictions that fail to categorize themselves and escape the warping influence of authorial intent." —*Electronic Book Review*

**Jackie Mallon** is the author of *Silk for the Feed Dogs*, published by Betimes Books in 2013.

She is an Irish writer and fashion designer currently living in New York. After studying at London's St. Martins School, she worked in the world of high fashion in Milan for eight years, stockpiling stories for her first novel.

"*Silk for the Feed Dogs* is a stellar accomplishment – get it, read it, you won't regret the indulgence of silk against your skin."

—*DisappearingInPlainSight.com*

**Donald Finnaeus Mayo** is the author of *Francesca*, published by Betimes Books in 2013.

He was born in London and grew up in Australia and South East Asia, the backdrop for his first novel, *Francesca*. At various times he has worked as a radio journalist for the BBC, a business writer, and as a photographer.

"Perhaps reading it prior to going to bed is not advisable as one might end up staying up rather later than one intends and arrive at work blurry eyed the next day."

—*Establishment Post, Singapore*

**Craig McDonald** is the author of *One True Sentence, Forever's Just Pretend, Toros & Torsos, The Great Pretender, Roll the Credits* and *The Running Kind,* published by Betimes Books in 2014.

He is an award-winning author and journalist. The Hector Lassiter series has been published to international acclaim in numerous languages and enthusiastically endorsed by a who's who of crime fiction authors. McDonald's debut novel was nominated for *Edgar, Anthony and Gumshoe awards* in the U.S. and the 2011 *Sélection du prix polar Saint-Maur en Poche* in France.

**Colin O'Sullivan** is the author of *Killarney Blues*, published by Betimes Books in 2013. O'Sullivan's short fiction and poetry have been published in various print and online anthologies and magazines, including *A Living Word* (anthology of Irish writers), *Staple New Writing, The Stinging Fly, These are Our Lives* and *Cork Literary Review.* He lives in the north of Japan and works as an English teacher.

"I read this novel and saw a movie in my mind – that's how each page appeared to me – and that's a good thing."

—*LoveSexAndOtherDirtyWords.com*

 **Kevin Stevens** is the author of *Reach The Shining River*, published by Betimes Books in 2014. He is the author of two novels published by Simon & Schuster UK, *Song for Katya* and *The Rizzoli Contract*, and *This Ain't No Video Game, Kid!*, a novel for young adults published by Little Island. His superhero fantasy for children, *The Powers*, is the Dublin UNESCO City of Literature Citywide Reading Project for children in 2014. Kevin lives in Dublin and Boston and writes about jazz and American politics for *The Irish Times* and other publications.

# ALSO PUBLISHED BY BETIMES BOOKS

ISBN: 978-0-9926552-6-6 1

ISBN: 978-0-9926552-2-8 1

ISBN: 978-0-9926552-1-1 1

ISBN: 978-0-9926552-7-3 1

ISBN: 978-0-9926552-8-0 1

ISBN: 978-0-9926552-9-7 1

ISBN: 978-0-9929674-0-6 1

ISBN: 978-0-9926552-8-0 1

ISBN: 978-0-9926552-9-7 1

ISBN: 978-0-9929674-0-6 1

ISBN: 978-0-9926552-0-4 1

ISBN: 978-0-9926552-3-5 1

ISBN: 978-0-9926552-4-2 1

ISBN: 978-0-9926552-5-9 1